CW0671451

THE SECRETS
of
SCHEHERAZADE

The Scheherazade Foundation

THE SECRETS
of
SCHEHERAZADE

The Scheherazade Foundation CIC
85 Great Portland Street
London
W1W 7LT
United Kingdom
www.SF.Charity
info@SF.Charity

First published by The Scheherazade Foundation CIC, 2022

THE SECRETS OF SCHEHERAZADE

The various authors listed above assert the right to be identified as the Authors of
the Work in accordance with the Copyright, Designs and Patents Act 1988.
A CIP catalogue record for this title is available from the British Library.

ISBN 978-1-915311-01-6

The wisest of queens, Scheherazade conjured magic,
woven from ordinary threads turned inside out.

Arabian saying

CONTENTS

The Ripening of Rustam Khan

Tahir Shah

ONCE UPON A time, long, long ago, when birds flew in zigzag lines and the moon was always full, a little boy was born to a swordsmith and his wife.

They named him Rustam Khan.

From the winter morning of his birth, the little boy yearned to make a difference, even before he knew there was a world beyond his crib.

As his first weeks slipped into months, and then beyond a year, Rustam Khan's yearning grew and grew.

While the other infants in the village were crawling about on their stomachs, the swordsmith's son was already imagining the things he was to do as soon as he could get up on his feet and walk.

Winter snows melted, giving way to spring. Then the blistering summer heat was replaced by the cold once again.

And still Rustam Khan yearned.

Each day, he would sit in a little chair beside the forge and watch his father hammering steel blades destined for the kingdom's warriors.

While other boys were thinking about stalking toads in the reeds, Rustam Khan spent every waking moment wondering what his lot was to be, and how he could be the very best version of himself.

Beneath a sprawling mulberry tree in the middle of the village, he learned to read, write, and count with the other children. Then, each day after lessons, he would help his father in the workshop, preparing the steel to be beaten into blades.

Seven winters came and went.

Then another seven.

'The day will come when you are a great swordsmith,' the boy's father said proudly one afternoon. 'Always remember that a fine sword is capable of being used for war or peace.'

That night, Rustam Khan went to bed, his father's words turning in his head. Rather than the usual dreams of gallant princes and endless battles, he found himself in a land where war was almost unknown.

Whenever two people had a quarrel, they would take up swords and settle their differences. But, unlike in the waking world, the swords on the dreamscape were ceremonial.

Their blunt blades were inscribed with messages of fraternity and peace. As the swords were swung, they radiated good energy. All at once, the differences were forgotten, and the quarrelling parties hugged as friends.

The morning after the curious dream, Rustam Khan attended his lessons under the mulberry tree, but his mind wasn't on what the teacher was saying. Instead, he was thinking about the magical swords he had seen in the dream world.

That afternoon, he went to his father's workshop as he always did, with the ceremonial swords still on his mind.

'What is troubling you, my son?' asked the swordsmith.

Rustam Khan described the dream.

'It was a world that was inside out,' he said in little more than a whisper.

The boy's father, who was holding a magnificent blade he had shaped over weeks, held the steel up to the light.

'Since I was your age, I have made swords in this workshop,' he said. 'Just as my father did, and his father before him.'

At that moment, the sound of horses' hooves could be heard charging down the valley. Rustam Khan and his father turned to see a cloud of swirling dust.

Within a minute or two, a knight of the realm was standing at the entrance to the workshop. Dressed in black, with an exquisite helmet replete with twin peacock plumes crowning his head, he held up a fabulous sword with a watered steel blade.

At once, the master swordsmith recognized it as a blade he himself had fashioned for the king.

'Did you not make this wretched weapon?' the knight demanded.

'I did indeed,' the swordsmith answered.

'Well, it has failed His Majesty! He's ordered that you are to be imprisoned in the deepest, darkest dungeon!'

Confused, the swordsmith held up a hand.

'That blade is the very finest ever to have been struck. Surely it did not fail in battle?'

The black knight shook his head.

'It was not used in battle,' he answered.

'Then, if I might enquire, how could it have failed His Majesty?'

'Because,' the knight replied, 'when His Majesty pulled back the scabbard and glimpsed his reflection, it displeased him.'

'May I remind His Majesty that it is a sword for battle, not a mirror for the boudoir.'

Within the blink of an eye, the swordsmith had been trussed up in chains and hauled away.

Rustam Khan begged for his father to be released, but the pleading went unheard.

As the swordsmith was dragged off, he cried out for his son to come close.

'Quick! Snatch the amulet from my neck!' he yelled. 'Hold it in your fist and let it lead you to the one person alive who can help me!'

Following the instructions, Rustam Khan tore away the silver amulet, and watched as the royal guard hurried back to the palace with his father as their prisoner.

Five minutes after the guard had gone, the dust settled. He wondered whether he had imagined the entire episode. But, as he stood there in shock, the little silver amulet began to warm in his fist.

Fearful at what fate his father would receive, Rustam Khan rushed home to his mother and explained what had happened.

'Your father has worn that amulet since he was a child,' she said, her expression grave. 'There is but one course of action. You must take to the open road and let it guide you.'

'But, Mother, how could an amulet like this guide anyone? After all, there are no directions or map.'

'Trust in it, my dear son. When it's warm to the touch, you will know you are on the right path.'

'And how will I know when I have reached the destination, Mother?' asked Rustam Khan, tears welling in his eyes.

'You will know because you know,' she replied. 'Now, take these provisions, and leave at once!'

And so, picking up a little knapsack filled with dried meat and fruit, the swordsmith's son set off to find the answer, the amulet in his fist.

From the first stride he made, it heated up, its warmth ebbing and flowing as though it were alive.

For days and then weeks, the young man kept going day and night.

The amulet's warmth guided him through forests and across mountains, over quicksand, and zigzagging through one kingdom after the next. And, as he ventured ahead, Rustam Khan was forced to survive by his wits, ripened by the journey.

From time to time the amulet cooled, signalling to Rustam Khan that he had deviated from the route he was supposed to take. He wondered whether he would ever reach an ultimate destination. But something coaxed him to keep going, despite all the odds.

A year and a day after setting out from the threshold of his home, Rustam Khan clambered up a mountainside. As ever, in his fist the amulet was pulsing with warmth.

All of a sudden, it grew hotter than it had ever been.

Panting from the climb, the wayfarer stopped in his tracks. He opened his fist and saw that the amulet was no longer silver, but was glowing with an eerie iridescent light.

Rather than radiating outwards in all directions, the light seemed to be pointing towards a cave.

Summoning his courage, Rustam Khan made his way to the cavern's mouth and shuffled inside. As his eyes adjusted to the darkness, he heard a voice… a woman's voice.

'I have waited for you,' it said.

'Who are you?!' the young man called out.

'I am the amulet that you hold in your hand.'

Rustam Khan looked down, and saw that the voice was indeed emanating from the amulet.

'But I have come on a long journey to find someone who can save my father. If you are the amulet that has guided me all these weeks and months, why haven't you spoken to me before?!'

'Because, as I said, my dear Rustam Khan, I have been waiting.'

'Waiting for me to reach this cave… up here on the mountainside in a distant kingdom?'

'No,' whispered the voice gently. 'I've been waiting for you yourself to be ready to save your father.'

Rustam Khan sensed his bloodstream coursing with adrenalin. He had travelled for a year and a day, while his father was surely being tortured in the palace dungeons.

Reading his thoughts, the amulet spoke:

'As your father used to tell you, a sword is only perfect when it has strength and flexibility. In the same way, to be effective, a young man must have the right qualities – qualities that can only come through experience. Without experience, no amount of youthful enthusiasm can succeed.'

Incensed at having been lured to the end of the earth, Rustam Khan held the amulet up and glared at it.

'So what am I to do?!' he yelled. 'Because, in case you have forgotten, my father is languishing in a dungeon… that is, if he's still alive.'

The amulet cooled, the stream of iridescent light fading.

Rustam Khan felt more alone than ever before.

Standing there in absolute darkness, he thought back to all the adventures he had experienced since setting off from the valley of his birth.

As he remembered the escapades, they were projected over the cave walls.

'You are ready,' said the voice. 'Listen with care.'

And, as Rustam Khan listened, the amulet explained what to do.

When he had committed the instructions to memory, he began to ask the amulet the route he should take back to the kingdom from which he had come. Before the question had left his mouth, he realized he was no longer in the cave on the mountainside.

Instead, Rustam Khan was now standing at the base of a great citadel.

Peering up, he perceived at once that it was the palace in which the cruel king resided – and where his father was imprisoned.

He was about to do as the amulet had bid him to do, when he heard a troop of the royal guard marching fast towards the gates. To his surprise, he saw they were the very same soldiers that had taken his father. Sure enough, as he watched, Rustam Khan spied his father being dragged inside the palace.

Through some feat of magic, the amulet had taken him back in space and time.

Waiting for the citadel's great doors to close, the young man hurried around to the rear of the palace, as he had been told to do.

As the amulet had said, he found a low doorway covered in foliage. In times of danger, it had been constructed as a direct route of escape for the royal family, and was long since forgotten.

Ten minutes after slipping through the concealed portal, Rustam Khan found himself in the king's private apartment. The walls were hung with the finest silks, the air scented with perfumes from the East.

The secret passage had circumvented the droves of armed guards who protected the royal family both night and day.

Hearing the sound of footsteps, Rustam Khan hid behind a curtain.

Furled up in an embroidered silk robe, the king strode into the salon and hovered at a bowl of fruits, before popping a plump-looking fig into his mouth. He was about to take another when there was a knock at the door.

Turning, he found his chief of staff – the black knight – standing to attention.

'Your Majesty,' he said, bowing, 'may it please you to hear that the wretched swordsmith has been arrested and is in the dungeons, as you desired.'

'In the deepest, darkest dungeon?' the monarch snarled.

'Yes, indeed, sire. The very deepest, and the very darkest of the dungeons.'

'And what of the damned sword?'

The black knight held it up.

'Here it is, Your Majesty.'

'Ten years in the dungeons will teach that lowly creature to make sure the royal reflection is always handsome!'

Placing the magnificent sword on a low divan, the black knight strode out, leaving the king alone.

In a single deft movement, Rustam Khan stepped out from behind the curtain, snatched the sword, and held it to the monarch's throat.

'Make a sound and I'll end your days,' he said. 'The blade may not please you as a mirror, but I assure you it's sharp enough to shave with.'

An hour after his son had slipped in through the secret doorway, the swordsmith had been rescued from the dungeons. In his place was the king, whimpering and forlorn.

An hour after that, Rustam Khan took the amulet from his pocket. He was about to tie it around his father's neck when he whispered a line of thanks.

To his surprise, the voice came again, as it had done in the cave.

'Why don't you thank me to my face?' it said.

As Rustam Khan stepped back, confused, a plume of smoke billowed out from the amulet. In less time than it takes to tell, it materialized into the most attractive young woman the swordsmith's son had ever seen.

'My name is Princess Leila,' she said. 'My father was deposed by the grandfather of the brutal monarch whom you have imprisoned.'

'You mean…?'

Leila nodded.

'My father was the king, and this was our palace.'

Bowing, Rustam Khan pledged his loyalty.

In the days that followed, Princess Leila assumed the throne, and was immediately as adored by her subjects as her own father had once been.

Given a royal warrant, the swordsmith found himself working from the finest workshops within the palace.

As for Rustam Khan, he used the experience he had gained from his adventure to make a fortune for himself, and for others. And, having travelled with him on his great adventure, and known firsthand that he was the finest man alive, the princess waited for the day when he was ready.

One spring morning, while they were out walking together in the valley where he had been born, Rustam Khan got down on one knee and asked Princess Leila to be his bride.

Her face glowing with unbridled delight, she accepted at once.

And that is how a young man, who had been born as a swordsmith's son in a time of woe, went on to be ripened, and to know true love.

The Lamp Who Went in Search of Magic

Jason Webster

ONCE UPON A time there was a silversmith who made lamps. All day he made lamps, beating them into shape in his workshop before placing them on a shelf in the window for sale.

One day, the silversmith made a lamp which was just the same as all the others. But as the lamp waited to be sold, it said to itself: 'I am no ordinary lamp. I feel myself to be special, different. I have heard stories of extraordinary lamps that can do magical things. It is my strong desire to become one of them. In fact, I am convinced it is my destiny: I will become a magic lamp!'

It so happened that someone walked into the silversmith's shop at that very moment and picked the lamp up and bought it.

Aha! thought the lamp to itself. Here is proof that I am special. Fate has set me on a path that will lead me to greatness. The way may be long and challenging, but I am more than up to the task, for a magic lamp I must become!

Everywhere it went, whenever it met others of its kind, the lamp would always ask the same question: 'How do I become a magic lamp? Please show me the way, for this is my life's goal.'

Now many lamps looked a bit askance when it said this. But others warmed to it. 'I, too, have heard of these famed magic lamps,' they would say. 'And I want to become one as well. We should stick together and create a brotherhood, for by combining our efforts we are bound to find a real magic lamp who can teach us its ways.'

Years passed like this, and the lamp travelled far and wide (for its owners were merchants who were frequently on the move). Often it was lucky in being able to journey in the company of its fellow seekers, and in all places they came to, whenever they met new lamps from different cultures and countries, they asked about how they might become magic lamps.

Finally, in a distant land, they met a shiny golden lamp encrusted with jewels who, when they approached with their usual question, answered: 'I am a magic lamp, and I can teach you how to become like me.'

At this, the lamp and its companions were overjoyed. After so many years' searching, they were on the brink of fulfilling their destiny, for surely this magnificent lamp (whose shine and appearance had impressed them all the moment they had seen it) was the very one they had been dreaming of finding for so long, the one who would make their wishes come true.

'Our path to you has been long and arduous,' they all cried. 'And we are so keen to learn! When can we start?'

'Soon,' promised the golden lamp. 'But first, I have become a little tarnished while I have been here waiting for you to find me; you must clean me.'

'Of course,' the lamps eagerly replied. 'And could you show us some magic?'

'All in good time,' said the golden lamp.

The cleaning process seemed to last an age – far longer than any of them had expected. When they had finished, they turned to the golden lamp and said: 'Now can you teach us?'

'Later,' the golden lamp said. 'For now, I want you to find new jewels to decorate me. You see how one or two of them have been lost over the years? In order to teach you, I myself must first be complete. Now off you go and find them for me.'

The other lamps were impressed by the great teacher's humility in showing its imperfections, and their belief in it was strengthened even further as they set off on their quest.

'When we return with the jewels, then it will display its powers to us, and will show us the way to become magic lamps ourselves,' they confided to one another.

The search for the jewels took even longer than the first task, yet finally, after many trials, the gems were secured and brought back to the golden lamp.

'Now can we learn your secrets?' the lamps eagerly asked.

'You are too impatient!' cried the golden lamp. 'And your impatience makes you unworthy.'

The lamps bowed their heads in shame.

'You have brought me new jewels,' the golden lamp continued, 'but they need to be set into my sides. Only then will I be complete.'

The student lamps were humbled by his wisdom and embarked on their new task. It was very difficult for them, and required much training and effort on their part, but eventually, after yet more time had passed, they were able to begin. The lamp of our story was given the job of placing a gem on the master lamp's lid. Yet as it got closer, it noticed something: a tiny chip on the lamp's side revealed a dull metal colour beneath where the gilt had gone. Scratching a little more, it realized that the whole of the 'golden' lamp was in fact the same.

All at once, the lamp's head began to spin as it realized that the 'master lamp' was no master at all. It wasn't even made of gold, for underneath the shiny exterior it was, in fact, made of nothing more than ordinary copper.

'You are no magic lamp,' it cried. 'You are a fraud!'

Distraught and confused, the lamp left the company of its fellow seekers and wandered off alone. For many years it was just another solitary household item with no sense of purpose in life. So great was its disappointment that it lost all faith: in itself, in magic, even in being alive.

Meanwhile, after so many years' trying to learn magic, and now cast into a pit of despondency, it had practically forgotten to do the one thing it had been made for: to give people light. The truth was that it had been getting steadily worse at this one simple task for many years, and had passed from one owner to another, its value dropping each time, until finally it woke up one day to find itself back at the silversmith's where its journey had begun so long before, cast into a pile of old, almost useless lamps destined for smelting down.

'Oh, woe is me!' cried the lamp. 'After such high hopes and such great beginnings, not only have I been deceived and betrayed, yet here I am, cast onto the heap of failure. My dream of becoming a magic lamp was nothing but a nightmare that has brought me to the sorriest of endings. I am nothing.'

At this, an elderly and tarnished old lamp on the shelf spoke.

'What is this talk of *magic* lamps?' it said. 'You are a lamp, and a lamp alone. What made you think that there was such a thing as a magic lamp? Or that you might even become one?'

The lamp looked up and recognized the old lamp who was speaking.

'But you,' it cried, 'were the one who told me stories of magic lamps in the first place. It was *you* who told those tales that set me off on my quest.'

'Perhaps,' said the old lamp, 'you need to hear them again.'

And so it began to tell the stories that the lamp had heard it recite so many years before: tales of kings and queens, of goblins and fairies, of magicians and witches, and of jinns and genies – some of whom, at times, could be coaxed out of ordinary oil lamps. At first the lamp refused to listen; the stories were, after all, the cause of all its misfortune. But the storyteller persisted, and as it repeated its tales, the lamp began to pay attention, more closely, until finally, after much time had passed, it felt that it knew them all and could retell them itself.

And on the day that the meaning of the stories finally became clear to the lamp, the silversmith leant down and picked it up from the pile, gave it a clean, and put it out for sale once more.

Today, now that it has stopped wanting to be something it can never become, the lamp is steadily getting better at doing what it was always meant to do: provide people with light.

As for the question of magic, it leaves that to others.

But is there magic to be found *inside* the lamp, you ask?

That is a very different question.

And the only answer is to rub it… and find out.

Nasrudin: Cat Currency

Tahir Shah

YET ANOTHER FINANCIAL meltdown had rocked the world's global markets, leaving Nasrudin with little confidence in established currencies.

So, he went to a butcher and spent all his money on sausages. From that day on he paid for everything in them, bartering on a system he had drawn up that was fair.

Those he met thought it was a little eccentric, but they expected nothing less from the wise fool, who had turned up in the city a month or so before. In any case, the sausages were delicious, and people were only too happy to eat them.

One night, having discovered the store of currency while its owner slept, Nasrudin's cat gobbled up his entire stock of sausages.

The wise fool was angry at the animal, but appeared as usual at the grocer's the next day.

When it was time to pay for the mountain of vegetables he had selected, the wise fool sniffed.

'I've changed currencies,' he said. 'I no longer pay in sausages.'

The grocer looked up at the customer sternly.

'Then what are you going to pay me in?'
'In a new currency.'
'And what is it?'
'It's called "the Cat".'

When the Sun Forgot to Rise

Tahir Shah

ONCE UPON A time, the herds of reindeer were so vast that when spied from the heavens by the great eagles of the frozen plains, they looked like ants.

The ground was so thick with ice that only the hardiest creatures survived the winter. And, as for human communities, they were few and far between. No one with any sense would endure what was known by one and all as 'The Great Darkness'.

Months passed in which there was almost no sunlight.

As one night slipped into the next, the people who endured the unendurable would huddle together and tell tales. Or rather, they would tell a single tale which roamed on and on, as endless as the arctic tundra beyond the wooden walls of the homestead.

The tale, passed down from one generation to the next, was sacred because it contained the collected wisdom of the tribe. Once it had been told from beginning to end, the first strains of spring sunlight would break out across the horizon.

Such was the length of the story – which was called the Tale of Elypsia – that only the elders of the community were permitted to recount it, for only they had committed to memory the many twists and turns, and all the details that were so central to the narrative.

Of all the elders, the finest at recounting the Tale of Elypsia was a woman who could remember the endless freezing, and the summer when the great mountains thawed.

She knew that the end of her days was coming, the time when she would forget the tale. Day after day, she spoke the story through the darkness.

And, as she did so, the next generation listened well, and they listened hard, because they knew that soon they would be required to pass on the tale as faultlessly to the youngers as had been done for them.

At last, her energy drained, her mind fading, the elder spoke the last sentence in a voice so frail it was barely heard at all:

'And then the queen drank the last of the mead, climbed onto her sleigh, and raced towards the sunrise.'

Everyone in the homestead, who had listened through the darkened days, applauded.

When their cheers had waned, one of the children, a little girl called Floria, ran to the window.

Wiping away the ice that caked the glass, she peered out into the curtain of black that shrouded the world in which they lived.

'The dawn should be here by now!' Floria called. 'It's supposed to be bright when the Tale of Elypsia is ended.'

The child's father touched a fingertip to his chin.

'Perhaps we ended a little sooner than usual this year,' he said with a smile.

'Let's wait until tomorrow,' Floria's mother said. 'It's sure to get light tomorrow.'

So, Floria, and all the others, waited.

They waited, and they waited.

And, they waited, and they waited.

They waited a night, and then a day…

…and they waited a week, and then a pair of weeks.

After that, they waited an entire month.

But still, sunrise did not come.

Concerned at the lack of sunlight and the effect it would have on the herd, Floria's father touched a fingertip to his chin once again.

'I wonder what could have happened,' he said.

Floria stared hard into his father's eyes and blinked.

'It's obvious,' she said. 'The sun has been asleep for so long that it's forgotten to rise.'

There was laughter as everyone enjoyed the words of the child.

When the laughter was over and silence prevailed, Floria spoke once again:

'Tomorrow I am going to venture out into the darkness,' she said, 'and I'm going to remind the sun to rise.'

Again, there was laughter.

And again, everyone enjoyed the words of the child.

Next morning, Floria was up before her brothers and sisters. Slipping on her clothes, she went to the window, brushed off the ice, and peered out once again.

Amazingly, it seemed even darker than before.

With her parents and all the other children still asleep, Floria put on her heavy coat and went to the door.

Then, feeling braver than she had ever felt before, she slipped outside.

The darkness was so gloomy that the little girl could hardly see where she was going. But gradually, her eyes became a little more accustomed to the darkness.

Weaving her way through the herd of reindeer, she made her way out from the encampment into the arctic wasteland that lay beyond.

As she walked, she told herself fragments of the story, the Tale of Elypsia, which she had listened to throughout the winter.

'One day,' she told herself, 'I will speak the tale better than it has ever been spoken. And when I do, the naughty sun won't dare stay asleep as it has done. It's not respectful! When I get to it, I'll give it a firm telling-off!'

All morning, Floria paced towards the end of the tundra, her boots scraping against the ice and her face frozen from cold.

She might have wished she had stayed at home in the warmth, but the Tale of Elypsia kept her going, as did the thought of scolding the sun.

Hours after leaving the homestead, Floria began to wonder where the sun would be. After all, it wasn't as though it would be hiding in a cleft in the rocks, or beneath a blanket of ice.

However far she walked, she couldn't get to the end of the land, to where the next horizon lay.

It was then that she had an idea.

Marching out in search of the sun was showing weakness.

If she was strong – a fearless little girl who wasn't afraid of scolding the sun – she would surely want the sun to come to her, rather than the other way around.

So, digging her heels into the ice, she refused to take another footstep.

Then, rubbing a hand to her chest to warm up her lungs, she yelled:

'You're a very, very naughty little sun, and you're to wake up at once! If you don't, I'll get very angry with you! Do you hear me?!'

Silence.

Silence… but for the distant roar of an avalanche.

Floria yelled a second time, far louder and more stridently than before.

But again, there was silence… except for one of the reindeers calling out far away.

Her heels still dug deep into the ice, Floria thought long and hard.

'If I was a naughty little sun that had fallen fast asleep,' she said to herself, 'what would it take to wake me?'

Thinking harder than she had ever thought of anything before, she thought of how her mother and father would beg her to get up on the deepest, darkest winter mornings… and how she would want to stay in bed. Most of all, she pondered, she hated it when they scolded her. The only way she would agree to get up out of her snug little bed was when her mother sang to her.

'That's what I'll do,' Floria said to her herself, 'I'll sing the sun awake!'

So, filling her lungs once again with frozen morning air, she sang and she sang…

…and she sang and she sang.

She sang of birds, of forests, and of rivers…

…and she sang of little chicks, of mountains, and of eagles high in the summer sky.

And, as she sang, something remarkable happened…

The faintest rays of sunlight warmed against the night sky and, slowly, began to break across the horizon.

Still Floria sang, her young voice charming the stream of light.

By now, the sunshine was so dazzling that the little girl's eyes were burning. Having jumped up and down with delight, she remembered her manners.

Calling out to the horizon, adorned with a glowing orb of gold, she yelled out:

'Thank you, dearest sun, for waking from your slumber, and for bringing beauty to our world! Every day that you shine above me, I'll thank you as I'm doing now. And, when you go to sleep again after working so hard through weeks and months, I'll remember to wake you. So don't worry about oversleeping, if it happens again!'

Then, her arms and legs throwing out the longest of shadows, Floria tramped home…

…to tell her family how it had been her who had woken up the sun.

Life in a Dead Man's Hand

Jason Webster

18 May 1868

Today has been a good day. An interesting day.

Digging resumed just after dawn. We decided to concentrate on the north-western corner of the site, in the shadow of the Montaña Verde. Over the past days the area has revealed a number of hollows in the ground – none of them significant in themselves, but collectively they seem to indicate human activity of some description. All of us with the same idea of what it might be, but none daring to say, for fear of jinxing the expedition.

Less than an hour in, Pablo called me over. An urgency in his voice alerted me immediately. I hurried across, and there…

But I need to start earlier than that, for I have just remembered the dream I had shortly before waking. Although 'dream' suggests that there were images of some kind. This was more about a sound, a drumming in my mind with a steady, hypnotic rhythm:

Da-da Da da, da Da da
Da-da Da da, da Da da

Da da DA da
Da da DA da

On and on it went, as if for hours, until words seemed to be added to it, like a chant. Even now, as I recall the experience, I can hear them quite clearly:

Ha llegado la hora
Ha llegado la hora
La semilla
La semilla.

'The time has come, the time has come, the seed, the seed.'

(How strange that I should remember this now, yet all through the day it was as if the dream had never existed.)

Back to this morning... Pablo pointed when I reached the spot, but it was if I already knew what I was about to see. The heads of a clutch of textile figures poked out from the dust. Beside them, skeletal remains over 400 years old of a member of the Chancay civilization's elite class. (Later, preliminary observations suggest they are those of a man in his thirties.)

I knelt down to take a closer look, my heart beating hard in my breast. This was, after all, what we were hoping to find: a burial site, and within the graves, examples of the mysterious 'dolls' said to have been interred with the dead.

I admit my hand trembled with excitement as I started to brush away the soil. Within minutes the figures began to reveal themselves: there were three of them, squeezed together in the left hand of the dead man, whose finger bones lay scattered in a halo beneath them like rays from the sun.

From behind, I heard Pablo mutter something: '*Suerte*' –
luck. Although whether he was celebrating the 'luck' of our
find, or wishing me luck (because he thought I was going
to need it), I couldn't be certain. Despite being a scientist,
occasional glimpses of a superstitious background appear in
him now and again.

Before luncheon, the figures had been released from the
Chancay's hand, dusted down as well as possible, and were
lying in a row on my table. They vary between six and ten
inches high and three to four inches across. From what
we know so far of their tradition, based on the distinctive
fashioning of their hair, they represent two females and one
male. The textiles of which they are made are in superb
condition, having suffered very little degradation in this
exceedingly dry soil. Inside, from what is visible where
the stitching has opened, they are stuffed with straw and
dried grass. It is my firm belief that they represent the best-
preserved examples of so-called Chancay burial dolls ever to
have been found – a point I shall be making very clear in the
paper I have been invited to give at the RGS on our return
to London.

And the colours! By God, how bright they are, even after
all these centuries in the ground. We may know precious
little about Chancay civilization (they were, after all,
annihilated by the Incas not long before Columbus), but
based on these figures alone one has to speculate that they
were a gay, fun-loving people.

I made notes quickly as I examined each one, conscious
that our midday break would soon be upon us, when tools

would be downed and the day's labour effectively ended (finding local help prepared to work more than four hours in a given day has proved a thankless task). I heard the familiar clang of the iron bell heralding the arrival of La Tuerta. This old hag is blind in her left eye, hence her nickname, 'the one-eyed woman'. Presumably she has a proper Christian name, but this is how all refer to her, and she seems not to mind. She comes every day to the site at the same time to sell cherimoya fruits to the site workers, and her arrival brings all archaeological tasks to a close as effectively as the setting of the sun.

By the time I reached her (for I, too, have succumbed to the delicious and invigorating charms of the local cherimoya fruit), she had clearly been informed several times of the day's great 'find' of the burial dolls.

'*Ha encontrado usted la vida*,' she said, as she relieved me of a handful of pesos. 'You have found life.'

'Life?'

'In the hand of *el muerto*. You have found life in the hand of the dead man.'

Something about her expression made me refrain from correcting her. She dropped the money into the front pocket of her apron (I am convinced she charges me more than the others), then mumbled words that I couldn't quite catch.

I asked her to repeat.

'I was asking permission,' she said. 'Permission to tell you,' she added, when she saw my confusion.

Which was when she told me. It is, of course, nothing more than local superstitious belief, of the kind that Pablo falls prey to at times. But I record it here for amusement, for posterity. Such material plays little part in the scientific approach, but it may, perhaps, be of anecdotal interest.

Here is what La Tuerta had to say:

These muñecas *are not, as you people think, mere 'dolls'. You think they come from this world. You think they were placed in the dead man's hand and buried along with him. But you are wrong. They are travellers from a land that you walk on each day, yet which you cannot reach. Not even your holes in the ground can reach their land, for they come from* el corazón de la tierra, *the Heart of the Earth. It is they who find and come to us; not us who make them, as you believe. And they bring with them a secret.*

(Here she paused. For a moment it was unclear whether she would carry on. She mumbled again; I urged her to continue.)

A secret (she said at last). *A secret so sacred and so big and so important that it can only be trusted to their kind.*

(Another long pause. In becoming a cherimoya seller, the woman, I thought, had missed her true vocation as a music hall performer.)

And do you know what they are trying to say? (She gave no time to answer what was clearly a rhetorical question.) *They are saying:* 'Siémbrame! Siémbrame!' *Sow me!*

Inside each one, deep inside its belly, buried in the straw and grass, there is a seed. But no ordinary seed. It is la semilla de la vida, *the Seed of Life. The Seed that restores Life to the Earth. Nothing less than Life itself!*

(At this point she dropped her basket of fruit, scattering them on the ground, and flung out her arms.)

*Not everyone can find the Seed, however. Some do not know
what it is. Others recognize it and grind it into flour to make
bread to eat. Only a few understand its true potential, and
sow it for those who will come after them. Yet such as these
come only once every thousand years.*

(A clue, perhaps – and one worth exploring – that these
figures represent some primitive fertility symbol, a promise
of rebirth in the face of death: a not uncommon idea within
underdeveloped societies.)

Yet there is a catch. (And here she leaned in closer to me,
her voice dropping to little more than a whisper.) *Only one
of them bears the true seed. Choose the right one, and plant
its sacred gift, and you will sow eternal Life. But choose the
wrong one, and destruction and decay shall be your only
harvest.*

*Now they are with you; you have stolen them from the hand
of the dead man. Life or death are for you to choose.*

How will you tell which is which?

And with this, she simply stopped, bent down to gather
her fruit, and walked away.

The Hoopoe's Flight

Tahir Shah

THERE WAS ONCE a little hoopoe.

When he hatched, his mother said:

'Never before has there been a chick as fine. He will grow into the king of all hoopoes.'

As for his father, his breast swelling with pride, he said:

'When my time here on the earth and in the firmament ends, may I be welcomed to the gates of Paradise for having sired such a fine son.'

Weeks passed, and the little hoopoe chick grew stronger and stronger, and his feathers grew sleek and radiant. From the first day that he took flight from the nest, perched as it was in a fissure between the rocks, all the other creatures in the sky cooed and cawed in delight at seeing such an exquisite bird.

But as so often happens in the realm of mortal creatures, other birds began to feel bothered that they were not quite as lovely as the hoopoe which, by this time, had been given the name Raye, which meant 'Magnificent'.

Months slipped by, and as they did so, a group of feathered creatures took to gathering at the water's edge in the last throes of dazzling afternoon sunshine.

'What are we going to do about him?' asked a scrawny crow angrily.

'We could peck out his eyes and leave him for dead!' suggested a falcon.

'Or we could all swoop into him as he's flying,' answered a thrush, 'so he careers into the rocks!'

Now, it just so happened that another creature was at the waterhole that evening. Unlike the birds, he didn't have feathers, a beak, or talons.

But he had travelled far and wide in his life… a life spent navigating the waterways of the kingdom.

He was an alligator.

'I have a suggestion for you,' he said in little more than a whisper.

An old buzzard, perched on a branch poking out of the water, let out a screech.

'Why should we, proud feathered creatures of the skies, listen to a scaly wretch like this? He can't even fly!'

A robin piped in, speaking for the others:

'Surely,' he said, 'in our desperate state, we need to listen to any ideas, irrespective of who or what speaks them.'

The other birds agreed and, huffing to himself, the buzzard fell silent.

'What's your suggestion, O Great Scaled Lizard of the Water?' asked an elderly owl.

The alligator raised his snout above the waterline.

Then, in a faint, raspy voice, he said:

'My suggestion is to do what we alligators do when we come across youngers with far too much energy and enthusiasm.'

'And what, pray tell, is that, O Scaled Lizard?' the owl probed.

'It is to present him with a wager. Tell him that you don't believe he can fly right up to the very top of the sky – higher than any bird has ever flown. It's what we do with cocky young alligators when they are too full of themselves... we bet they can't swim down through the river and touch the bottom.'

'And what happens to them, your young alligators?' asked a heron.

'They are reminded that they may be young, but they are lacking in experience,' answered the alligator.

The birds thanked the alligator and set off to find Raye, the little hoopoe. When they were sure the little bird's parents were nowhere to be seen, the owl flapped over to the nest.

After greeting the handsome young hoopoe, the owl said:

'Hello, Master Hoopoe, I happened to be passing. And as I passed, I wondered.'

'What did you wonder, Old Owl?'

'I wondered whether a hoopoe has ever flown right up to the top of the sky before. I assume one has not, but, as an intelligent bird, such questions interest me.'

The little hoopoe felt his muscles tingling.

Without wasting a moment, he took the deepest of breaths and shot straight up into the air.

Wings flapping double speed, he reached higher than the tops of the trees… then higher than the tallest mountains…

Up, up, up…

…until he was higher than any hoopoe had ever flown before.

But still the little hoopoe soared heavenward.

Up… up… up… wings flapping, his lungs panting as his muscles burned.

Far down below, the owl and the other birds watched.

'He's very high now,' said a thrush.

'I can hardly see him,' the robin broke in.

'Surely he'll freeze to death,' a kestrel squawked.

Up above in the heavens, the little hoopoe was indeed in danger of freezing. His feathers were so frozen that they were stiff, and his crest was covered in ice.

But still he flew on…

Up… up… up…

Until he could see the curvature of the atmosphere.

By this point, the air was so thin that the little hoopoe found himself entering a kind of dream state. Rather than passing out, he noticed he was able to perceive ideas in a way that they had been impossible to perceive before.

His little wings still flapping, he watched himself from a distance and remembered Old Owl challenging him as he had. And as he flapped, his body colder than cold, he saw what was happening.

'The other birds don't like me because I am young and fresh,' he thought to himself. 'They think I'm brash and all-knowing, and that I need ripening. So they're trying to hurt me. They are right that I am raw and unripened – of course

I am… because I'm young and have so little experience. But my youth means that I can find a path that's different to the paths they have all taken… a new path leading to new destinations.'

At that moment, just as Raye, the little hoopoe, was about to freeze to death, he saw something floating just above him. In his weakened state, he wondered whether it was the heavens.

His mind reeling, wings too frozen to flap any longer, he collided with the object and passed out.

The little hoopoe had no way of knowing that what in actual fact had occurred, was that he had flown into a high-altitude balloon, which was attempting to break a record for no good reason at all.

Dressed in a space suit, one of the pilots spotted the frozen little bird, scooped him up in his gloved hand, and took him beside the heater.

Having climbed to the edge of space, the balloon began to descend. As it did so, Raye came to.

A short time later, the craft lowered through the atmosphere and the heavens, until it was level with the mountains, and then below the tops of the trees.

As the balloon descended, the little hoopoe, now warmed and more energetic than ever, stood on the outer rail of the gondola and thanked the universe for such a fine adventure.

'A few hours ago I was a young hoopoe without any experiences to my name,' he said to himself. 'But now, all thanks to Old Owl and his friends, I have travelled to the edge of space, and been challenged more than any other hoopoe alive!'

That evening, back in his family's nest, Raye regaled his parents with the tale of his journey.

'Old Owl and the other birds were so kind to me!' he squawked. 'They saw that I was raw and unripened, and they helped me to have an experience that would make me stronger!'

The mother and father hoopoe exchanged a troubled glance. After all, they knew full well what the other birds were thinking.

The mother was about to say something when the little hoopoe cocked his head back and peered up at the full moon.

'This morning I imagined that I'd spend my life flapping around the mountains and the trees,' he said. 'But now, thanks to Old Owl and his friends, I've seen there's nothing to stop me achieving the impossible... all I have to do is to believe in those of little faith.'

The Happiest Man in the World

Idries Shah

A YOUNG MAN who existed in comfortable enough circumstances sought out a certain wise man who was living in seclusion and was reputed to have all knowledge.

The youth said to him:

'Great Sage, I have no material problems, and yet I am always unsettled. For years I have tried to be happy, to find an answer to my inner thoughts, to come to terms with the world. Please advise me as to how I can be cured of this malaise.'

The sage answered:

'My friend, what is hidden to some is apparent to others. Again, what is apparent to some is hidden to others. I have the answer to your ailment, though it is no ordinary medication. In order for the prescribed treatment to work as it is meant to work, you must follow my directions to the letter, do you understand?'

'Tell me what it is, and I shall do exactly as you bid, O Master.'

'Very well,' the sage replied. 'You must set out on your travels, seeking someone in particular.'

'Who?'

'The happiest man in the world.'

'But why?'

'Ask not questions. Instead, listen to the directions and follow them as you have agreed. When you find the happiest man in the world, you must ask him for his shirt.'

'His shirt?' echoed the youth.

'Yes, his shirt.'

'And then what should I do?'

'You must put it on.'

Leaving the sage to silent reflection, the seeker began his search for happy men.

Through weeks and months, he followed a zigzagging route through kingdoms near and far. Each time he met a happy man he quizzed him, asking whether he was the happiest man in all existence. Each interview ended with the same inconclusive result:

'It is very true that I am happy,' he would be told, 'but as I understand it, there is someone even happier than me living beyond the next horizon.'

The seeker's journey snaked north and south, east and west, taking in the farthest reaches of the known world. As he travelled, he learnt customs of distant lands, new languages, fragments of irresistible detail, and folklore. Little by little, he was matured by incident and experience. Despite frequently questioning the merit in continuing such a seemingly futile search, something goaded him on…

…and on.

Months turned to years, and still he travelled, until he felt there was no inch of highway or byway on which he had not already trodden. Every happy man in existence had been quizzed at least once and had directed him elsewhere.

The young man – who was no longer quite so young – resigned himself to failure. Cursing the sage for sending him on such a wild goose chase, he acquiesced to begin the long journey home at dawn.

That night he sought refuge in a caravanserai at the edge of a great forest.

Before turning in for the night, he got chatting to a fellow wayfarer. As is the way in such places, the traveller enquired the purpose of the seeker's quest.

'I am searching for the happiest man in the world,' the youth replied. 'I have searched all points of the compass, and have resigned myself to failure.'

Sipping a cup of green tea, the fellow traveller peered deep into the campfire.

'On my own explorations I came across a man who was exceptionally happy,' he revealed. 'So happy was he that those who he encountered regarded him as a fool.'

'Tell me where he lives and I shall go to him without delay.'

The wayfarer passed on the directions:

'Traverse the red desert, then the blue mountains, and you shall reach the jade-green sea. Fashion a boat from driftwood and row yourself to the heart-shaped island beyond its southern shore. In a forest there, the happiest man in the world resides.'

Thanking the traveller, the seeker set off at first light.

First, he crossed the red desert with its blistering sands.

Then, he scaled the blue mountains with their infernal lightning and ice storms.

At last, he reached the jade-green sea – exactly as the wayfarer in the remote caravanserai had described.

Crafting a little boat from driftwood gathered on the southern shore, the youth rowed out to the island.

After being battered to and fro by punishing waves, he reached the coast. Dragging the craft onto the beach, he began searching for the happiest man in the world.

Exhausted, he staggered into the dense forest that covered much of the island. Eventually he emerged in a clearing, having lost his bearings more than once.

To his surprise, he spied a log cabin in the distance, smoke curling up from the chimney.

More surprising still was not the sight, but rather the sound.

For coming from the cabin was the rip-roaring bellow of a man laughing – the kind of laugh the young seeker had not heard in all his travels.

Approaching gingerly, he paced forward until he was at the building's door.

So pronounced was the laughter that the ground seemed to shake.

The youth knocked, but no reply was forthcoming.

So he pushed the door open.

Inside, he found a wizened old man sitting cross-legged on the stone floor, a voluminous turban wound tight around his head. He was laughing so hard that tears were rolling down his cheeks.

Awestruck by the sight, the seeker reached out a hand and tapped the laughing man on the knee.

'This may sound foolhardy, but many years ago I was sent by a sage on a quest to locate the happiest man in the world. Am I to believe you are he?'

Still laughing, the ancient replied:

'Yes, I am indeed the happiest man in all existence!'

'What excellent news!' the youth countered. 'Please do me the honour of giving me your shirt so that I myself may put it on.'

At hearing the request, the laughing man laughed all the harder, until the tears pooled on the flagstones beneath him.

'If you had taken a moment to inspect the situation with care,' he said, still howling with laughter, 'you would have noticed that I am not wearing a shirt at all!'

The youth did a double take.

The wizened figure was indeed speaking the truth – he was shirtless.

Disconsolate, the seeker bowed his head low and prepared to leave. As he did so, the laughing man unfurled his turban, allowing it to coil down onto the floor.

Squinting in confusion, the young man realized at once that the laughing man was none other than the sage who had sent him on the quest in the first place.

'O Master, if you were the one I have been seeking all along, why did you not reveal yourself as such at the very start? By doing so you would have surely saved me from years of hardship, experience, and adventure.'

His laughter dissipating into an ear-to-ear grin, the sage riposted:

'Because the journey was the first part of your treatment.'

'How so?'

'A raw man requires ripening before he is in a ready state to absorb what needs to be passed on.'

The seeker's eyes welled with tears.

'I am certainly ripened,' he replied forlornly. 'Seasoned through trial and tribulation, having crossed half the known world.'

'I can see it in your face,' the sage responded kindly. 'Now sit down beside me, and prepare to learn.'

Outrunning the Reaper

Tahir Shah

HAKIM, THE SON of Hakim, was descended from a long line of merchants. He prided himself on being the shrewdest trader alive – from his home in Marrakech, to distant Samarkand.

Year after year, Hakim bought cheap and sold high, making himself a vast fortune in the process. Everyone in the bazaars of the East knew that he – Hakim, the son of Hakim – was the most wily merchant in the world.

In markets and in office blocks, in tented desert encampments and in city restaurants, many tongues spoke of the business mind of Hakim, the son of Hakim. Others, jealous of his exceptional skill at turning a profit even in the most unlikely of situations, copied him. And they too made fortunes for themselves.

Now, it just so happened that the business community were not the only ones whose ears had heard of Hakim, the son of Hakim.

You see, every conversation spoken wafts up into the heavens and down to the nether regions of hell. And so it was that, as time passed, and as Hakim's fortune swelled to new and extraordinary dimensions, Death came to know of his vast accumulated wealth.

Although there is no way of knowing the intricacies of the system, it happened that Death appeared early one morning in a little teahouse on the edge of Marrakech.

Seated at a table in the shadows of the same establishment was Hakim, the son of Hakim. He was sipping a glass of sweet mint tea, thinking of a shipment of spices from Arabia, when he spotted Death six feet away.

Dressed from head to toe in black, she held a scythe in one hand and, in the other, she was clutching a sundial.

As the merchant's gaze fixated upon her, Death urgently inspected the sundial. She seemed gravely concerned, as though her calculations were somehow awry.

Terrified to the core, Hakim, the son of Hakim, leapt up and fled.

He clambered into his car, and he raced at full speed to Casablanca, in a desperate bid to put distance between him and the Grim Reaper.

Perspiring and bewildered, he arrived at his brother's home in the old medina. Having exchanged salutations with his brother, Hakim, the son of Hakim, explained what had happened.

The merchant's brother calmed his kith and kin, then served coffee.

But as Hakim took a sip of the beverage, he once again saw Death standing there.

Again, she was armed with a scythe and was fumbling with a sundial, seemingly more confused than before.

Letting out a shriek of woe and consternation, Hakim, the son of Hakim, leapt up and clambered into his vehicle once again. Uncertain how to out-pace the Grim Reaper, he drove straight to the airport and boarded a plane bound for New York.

With no luggage, or firm travel plans, he hurried to a car rental counter and asked for the fastest vehicle in their fleet. But, to his horror, Death was standing in the shadows, scythe and sundial in hand.

Once again, she seemed utterly confused.

More fearful than he had ever been in his entire life, Hakim, the son of Hakim, ran to the rental car, jumped in, and drove as fast as he could.

By sunset, he had reached a sleepy little town called Tinicum, well off the beaten track.

Letting out the heaviest sigh of his life, he checked into a motel.

A little calmer now, Hakim the merchant lay on the bed and thanked providence for sparing him. Just as the thanks left his lips, he felt a frozen chill sweep through the room.

Death was standing in the corner, scythe and sundial in hand as before.

This time, rather than appearing confused, she was smiling from ear to ear.

Realizing his time had come, Hakim, the son of Hakim, cleared his throat and asked the Grim Reaper why she seemed so content.

Pointing a finger to the sundial, Death replied:

'When I saw you earlier today, first in Marrakech, then in Casablanca, and after that at the airport in New York, I was so confused.'

Plucking up courage, the merchant enquired why.

'Because,' answered Death, the blade of the scythe raised above her head, 'I knew I had a rendezvous with you here in Tinicum, at this exact appointed hour.'

The Berber Queen and the Necklace of Fortune

Jason Webster

ONCE THERE WAS a Berber queen who ordered that a necklace be made for her.

'It should be neither too beautiful,' she said, 'nor too plain. Neither too big nor too small. Yet it should be able to last for many, many lifetimes.'

A royal command was issued that all the jewellers in the land should present their work at the court within the space of a month and a day.

When the time passed, the jewellers duly arrived and showed the queen the necklaces they had made for her, hoping to win her favour. But each one was either too extravagant, encrusted with gems and shining gold, or too large and would almost crush her with its weight.

'No no no,' said the queen. 'None of these are what I asked for.'

Finally, an old jeweller – the first in the queue yet the last to be shown through to the queen – exhibited his piece of work. It was delicate and exquisitely made, yet strong and had neither gold nor jewels. At once the queen placed it around her neck and smiled.

'Yes,' she said. 'This is the one. Henceforth, this shall be the Royal Necklace. Whoever owns it shall be monarch of this land. But beware, for such a fate can be a blessing or a curse for those who wear it.'

Now, for many years the necklace was passed down through generations of the queen's family, and while it did so, the kingdom was at peace. One day, however, a courtier greedy for power decided that he should be the bearer of the necklace. And so in the dead of night he crept into the palace and stole it.

Sure enough, in a very short time, he rose to power and became king. And people remembered the original words of the queen who had had it fashioned so many years before: the necklace itself must have special properties, for its wearer now sat on the throne. Some called it the Necklace of Fortune; others, the Necklace of Power.

Under the new ruler, the kingdom became an unhappy place: crops failed, people went hungry, there was anger and resentment in the cities. Eventually a neighbouring power invaded and destroyed it. The king was killed in battle, and the palaces and cities razed to the ground.

Many years passed.

Tales of the former kingdom and the necklace were almost forgotten. One day, tending her sheep in the ruins of the palace gardens, a young shepherdess heard an unusual cry from one of her flock.

On going to investigate, she saw that the poor animal had caught its teeth on something strange. Untangling it and pulling it out from the soil, she held up something she had only ever heard of but never seen: a necklace. Dusting it off and peering at it closely, she saw that it was beautifully crafted, and instinctively she lifted it up and placed it around her neck.

As she did so, she seemed to hear a voice, as if from nowhere, speak to her: 'Beware this necklace: it can bring great fortune, but also great misery. Be careful how you use it, and who you give it to.'

The young shepherdess wondered for a moment if she had gone mad, but she decided nonetheless to keep the necklace, hiding it, as a precaution, inside her undergarments.

With time, her flock prospered and grew. Their wool always commanded very high prices at market, and soon it became the most sought after in the land. The shepherdess grew wealthy, and with wealth came power. Her country became important again, and in time was declared a kingdom once more. And placed at its head was none other than the shepherdess herself, a new Queen of the Berbers. At her coronation she revealed for the first time the necklace that adorned her breast. The ancient stories of the Necklace of Fortune were revived: here was proof, if such were needed, that it did indeed hold great power.

Now the queen, everyone said, needed a husband to ensure that the royal line could continue. So word was sent out that suitors should present themselves at court to try to woo her. And the queen, remembering the warning she had heard when she first found the necklace, made arrangements.

Soon suitors presented themselves one by one at the palace – sons of the great and the good from all over the land.

With each one, the queen behaved in the same way: after greeting them and making them welcome in her home, she made sure they caught sight of the Royal Necklace, placed on the shoulders of a mannequin in her bedchamber. And no sooner was her back turned and the suitor thought the coast was clear, than each one in turn pulled the necklace from the doll and tried to make off with it… only to be seized by guards waiting on the queen's orders.

Suitor after suitor fell into disgrace, caught out in the same way. Time passed, months turned into years, and still the queen had not found a husband. The people began to worry.

Then one day a young man, a son of no one, arrived at the palace and declared that he had come seeking the queen's hand. The courtiers laughed at his rags and demeanour, but the queen ordered him to be sent in.

'Have you forgotten,' she told her ministers, 'that I, too, was just a humble shepherdess not so long ago?'

The young man presented himself, and he was neither handsome nor plain, neither too big nor too small.

'I come bearing nothing but myself,' he said. 'For myself is all I have in this world.'

The queen was pleased by him and took him into the privacy of her bedchamber. There, as before, the Royal Necklace had been draped over the mannequin, but the young man barely noticed it.

'Do you know what that is?' asked the queen, pointing to it.

'I have heard stories,' answered the young man.

As before, the queen made her excuses and left her suitor alone in the room. Outside, as was their command, the guards in their positions waited. And waited. No sound came from inside.

Eventually the queen herself went inside to investigate: there was the necklace still on the mannequin's shoulders, while the young man sat calmly on a cushion drinking tea.

That very day, the couple were married. And the next morning the queen spoke to her newlywed.

'For centuries,' she said, 'this necklace has driven men mad with a lust for power, yet by choosing me over it you have proven yourself worthy. You are now my husband and as such, king of this land. The necklace must now rest on your shoulders.'

And with this she went to lift the necklace from the mannequin and place it around his neck.

But her husband backed away.

'Madam,' he said, 'you are queen – *my* queen. For me, that is enough. I have no need to become king, nor for the necklace nor its power. It is yours and yours alone.'

'Oh my husband,' said the queen with tears in her eyes. 'Know that this necklace was both a blessing and a curse, and had the power to bring great fortune to those who deserved it, and misfortune to those who did not. Now, however, your kindness has broken its spell and it is just a necklace once more. By your goodness of heart, its power has gone.'

The queen and her husband lived happily thereafter and brought stability and happiness to the kingdom. And their line continued after them for many generations.

As for the necklace, for many years it was forgotten. Soon the stories about it were told no more, as if they had never been told in the first place. Eventually it was given away to a poor man who sold it and was able to make a better life for himself. Thereafter it passed through many hands, just another necklace, like so many others.

Yet there are those who remember, who whisper the tale of the Royal Necklace in only the most secret of places and on the most unique of occasions.

And they say that if the necklace and its own story are ever reunited, then its extraordinary powers may one day be restored...

Nasrudin and the Lost Key

Tahir Shah

EVERYONE WHO KNEW Mulla Nasrudin was well aware of his many phobias.

No one, it seemed, had more fears than the wise fool.

Nasrudin was frightened of spiders and lizards, of dogs, cats, scorpions, and bears. As if that wasn't enough to deal with, he was frightened of the wind and the rain, of any vehicle with wheels, and of his own shadow.

But there was one phobia that was more pronounced than any other.

A fear of the dark.

And so it was all the more surprising when, late at night, Nasrudin was found near his own home searching under a street lamp for something in the dirt.

He had already been looking for more than an hour when a neighbour stopped on his way home.

'What are you doing, Nasrudin?' he asked. 'After all, I thought you were terrified of the dark.'

'I am! I am!' the wise fool barked. 'I'm usually tucked at home in bed by this hour. As everyone knows, darkness has a way of slipping in through the nostrils… and, when it's got into you, it's impossible to ever get out.'

The neighbour wasn't surprised to hear the mulla spouting such nonsense. After all, Nasrudin was widely regarded as the most foolish man alive. But, curious by nature, he asked again why he was crouched on the ground, searching.

'It's my door key!' the wise fool exclaimed. 'I've been searching for it for ages and can't find it.'

Although he wanted to get home, the neighbour got down on his hands and knees and helped to look.

A little time passed, and another neighbour stopped on his way home from the teahouse. He, too, asked what they were searching for.

'For Nasrudin's key,' the first neighbour explained. 'He's dropped it.'

Even though he didn't want to help, the second neighbour got down on his hands and knees and joined the search.

A little while after that, a third and a fourth neighbour stopped, and they all got involved in the hunt for the missing key.

Hours passed…

…hours in which multiple good-hearted neighbours searched.

The crescent moon high, and finding himself suddenly frightened of the dark, Nasrudin told the others that he had to rest from searching for a while.

The neighbours were piqued at seeing the mulla sit on the ground and take a long break.

Irritated beyond words at what seemed like a futile search, the first neighbour asked where exactly the wise fool had dropped the key.

Nasrudin pointed to a dark patch of scrub outside his home, a short distance away.

'Over there,' he said limply.

'Then why on earth are we all looking for the damned key over here?!' bawled the second neighbour.

'I would have thought it was obvious,' Nasrudin said sharply. 'You see, there's so much more light here under the street lamp.'

The King, the Dog, and the Golden Bowl

Idries Shah

ONCE UPON A time, there lived a merchant called Hassan, who was wealthy, happy, and blessed with good fortune.

But one day, disaster struck.

Laden with treasure from afar, his fleet of ships was captured by pirates. At the same moment, his warehouses – filled floor to ceiling with precious merchandise – were razed to the ground.

Unable to face his friends, Hassan sold his remaining belongings and set off in search of his fortune.

While he was asleep in a caravanserai, a thief stole his remaining money, and he found himself in an unfamiliar country without a single coin to his name.

Unsure of what to do, Hassan took refuge at a mosque, although ashamed of himself for having been reduced to the status of a beggar. Wondering how he was ever to hold his head up again, he asked the mosque-keeper for advice.

'My brother,' said the old man, 'go three days' march from here, and you will arrive at such-and-such a place. The king there is both generous and kind. You may be able to put your case before him. He will certainly help in a more substantial way than we can here at the mosque.'

Fishing out a handful of coins from the poor-box, he passed them to the beggar with God's blessing.

Sincerely thankful, Hassan set off.

The way was arduous, and by the time he reached the walls of the city where the generous king was said to live, Hassan was tired, thirsty, and famished. Staggering through the streets, he saw that the shopkeepers were richly clad, and everyone appeared well fed, content in body and mind.

Wearily, Hassan made his way towards the palace, where the mosque-keeper had said the generous fed the hungry each night.

But when he finally arrived at the magnificent building, Hassan was overcome with shame. He was shoeless and dressed in rags. Fearful of presenting himself in such a state before the monarch, he hid behind a pillar.

From that vantage point, he surveyed the scene.

In the middle of the palace was a concourse of people, young and old, each one of them being given food and money from the hand of the kind-hearted king.

From his hiding place, Hassan spied three great hounds being brought to a space a few feet away from him. An attendant placed a bowl of the finest meat on the floor – one for each of the hunting dogs.

The attendant strode away, leaving the animals to feast.

When he was gone, Hassan found his eyes fixed upon the delicious meat on which the hounds were feeding. His mouth drooling, he imagined the taste of the meat.

As he watched, the dog nearest to him raised its eyes to his and, looking at him in an almost human fashion, shoved its jewelled golden bowl towards Hassan with his nose.

Starving, the impoverished merchant helped himself to a large, succulent morsel of meat, before pushing the bowl back to the hunting dog.

But with its paw, the animal again nudged the vessel over to Hassan, apparently coaxing him to eat to his heart's content. Only when the beggar had eaten to bursting did the animal polish off what was left. Once he had licked the bowl clean, he prodded it back towards Hassan with the tip of his nose.

The dog was offering him the golden bowl.

Taking it in his hands, Hassan hid the precious object under his tattered cloak. Watching, the hound seemed to nod his head with approval.

Hassan knew full well that, were he to sell the bowl and buy himself new clothes, he would have a chance to rebuild his life.

Patting the dog gratefully on the head, he slipped out of the palace, where the generous king was still feeding those in need.

Next day, Hassan sold the exquisite bowl. Being studded with precious jewels, it brought him in such a good price that he was able to set up in business for himself.

By shrewd buying and selling, he soon had enough merchandise to take back to his native country, where his friends greeted him with much celebration and joy.

Good luck having returned to Hassan's life, he became a successful trader once again. Before long he was wealthier than he had ever been.

Years passed, but he never forgot the kindness of the dog that gave him the golden bowl.

One day, spurred on by gratitude and a sense of duty, Hassan made up his mind to replace the precious object he had been given by the hound.

Working with the best craftsman in the kingdom, he designed a perfect replica. Within days the bowl was ready.

Once dressed in flowing robes and in boots of the finest leather, Hassan mounted his most magnificent horse and set off.

After many adventures, he reached the ancient city walls that encircled the capital of the generous king.

But, riding through the imperial gates, he saw the city's houses were wrecked, silent and empty; the shops where rich and contented merchants had sat were despoiled of all their merchandise.

All the city's inhabitants were gone.

Worst of all, the great palace was wide open to the sky, roofless and ruined, its beautiful pillars crushed along with everything else, as if ravaged by Mongol hordes.

Sorrowfully, Hassan mounted his stallion to ride away. As he tugged the reins, a great hound darted fast from the ruins, followed by two more.

At once, Hassan recognized them as the fine hunting dogs that had once feasted from golden bowls, and helped a beggar in terrible need.

A few minutes passed, then an old man appeared. Wearing a rough woollen robe, he clasped the end of a stick in his hand.

'Greetings, my son,' he said. 'What brings you to this desolate place?'

Hassan returned the greeting, and explained:

'Some time ago I came here in rags and was fortunate enough to be given the meat from a bowl by this dog here. When I left I took the bowl, sold it, and replenished my fortunes. Now I have come to repay the debt and return an exact copy of the bowl.'

'Those times are gone,' said the ancient, 'and the vanity and pomp which was once my court has vanished, too.'

Squinting, Hassan saw that he was speaking to none other than the generous king whom he had seen feeding the poor with his own hand.

'Your Majesty,' said he, 'please take this golden bowl which I have brought.'

The old king chuckled.

'I have no need for anything,' he replied, 'except that which I have here. My hounds catch game for my one daily meal. And the palace gardener, who has remained with me, continues to grow vegetables for me. Together with the hounds we manage to enjoy our lives. After my enemies destroyed my town and my people were taken away, I have lived very simply here.'

'But... but... the bowl, the golden bowl,' uttered Hassan. 'May I not leave it for Your Majesty?'

'If a dog of mine thought fit to give away his bowl,' said the king, 'it is not for me to take it back. I am sure that he has no need of it now. Go, return from whence you came, we are sufficiently provided for at the present time.'

So, bowing low, Hassan mounted his steed and rode away. Looking back, he glimpsed the old king leaning upon his stick, waving a last farewell. A moment later, the old man had disappeared into the ruins, his hounds about him.

Riding day and night, Hassan reached his own country as quickly as he could. Deeply moved by the generosity, he set about liquidating his fortune, except for what he required to live a modest existence.

Then, calling upon the craftsman who had made the replacement bowl, he commissioned fifty more bowls – each one as splendid as the first.

When they were ready, Hassan gave the bowls to his most trusted retainers. Instructing them to take them far and wide, he gave orders for the bowls to be given to the misfortunate, so that they might rebuild their lives, as he himself had done.

Each of the bowls was inscribed with a story...

The Tale of the King, the Dog, and the Golden Bowl.

The Cap of Invisibility

Tahir Shah

ONCE UPON A time, a widow named Fatima was spinning wool in her cottage on the edge of the forest when a spider descended from the rafters and climbed over the yarn.

Noticing the arachnid, Fatima brushed at it.

As her fingers touched it, the spider swung away on a silken thread and was soon back in the shadows. Tut-tutting to herself, Fatima ran a hand up and down the yarn, hoping to clear away any trace of a web.

What the spinner had not realized was that, rather than brushing the silk away from the wool, she was in actual fact brushing it into the yarn.

Without giving it any thought, she carried on with her spinning and, by the end of the afternoon, she had enough wool prepared to knit her husband the cap he had been asking for.

Next morning, Fatima made breakfast for her children and bustled them out of the house for school. Once silence prevailed, she went over to her chair and picked up the balls of wool she had spun the day before.

But, to her unease, the yarn was glistening in spider silk.

Cursing herself for not keeping the house spic and span, she once again brushed the silk away. At least, that's what she thought she was doing. In actual fact, she was again brushing the fine gossamer of spider silk into the wool.

With the wind whipping through the trees outside, Fatima got down to knitting. And within an hour or two, she had almost finished the cap. Holding it up to the light, she admired the colours and the shape, imagining how pleased her husband would be when he came home from chopping wood in the forest.

Late that afternoon, the children trooped in from school. The youngest, a little boy named Hashim, raced over to the knitting and when no one else was looking, he pulled on the cap.

At the very same moment, the cat upset a pan of milk on the stove. Fatima rushed to the kitchen, shooed away the animal, and got down to mop up the spill.

Then, when order reigned once again, she called her children around and explained that they would all surprise their father with the fine new cap she had knitted.

'But where is the cap, Mother?' asked Leila, the oldest child.

'It's there, on my chair.'

'Where?'

Fatima flustered about, wondering if the cat had dragged it onto the floor.

'That doesn't make sense,' she said.

'And where's little Hashim?' asked the second daughter.

Clasping her hands to her cheeks, Fatima called out for the youngest one.

'Are you sure he came home from school with you all, my dears?'

'Yes, Mother!' the three daughters called out as one.

'Well, where could he have got to?'

Leila pointed to the chair, where a single ball of wool was sitting on the cushion.

'I saw him running over there, to–'

'To put on your father's new woollen cap!' Fatima broke in.

Just then, a shrill giggle was heard coming from behind the divan.

'Hashim?! Are you hiding there, you little rascal?!' the boy's mother cried. 'Come out at once!'

'But I *am* here,' Hashim said.

'Well, if you're there, why can't we see you?' snapped Leila.

'Where's the new woollen cap I've just knitted for your father?'

Tugging it off his head, Hashim held it out at arm's length. Instantly, he was visible, standing before the others.

Fatima and her daughters looked on in consternation.

'What work of a jinn is this?!' she exclaimed.

Shaking, Leila shared her grave fear, that her little brother was possessed.

Fatima reached forward. In a single movement she grabbed her little son, giving him the strongest hug, as though they had been apart for a lifetime and a half.

Her mind working at making sense of what had occurred, Fatima spoke:

'My grandmother once told me,' she said in less than a whisper, 'of a kind of spider that wove a special web.'

'What kind of web, Mother?'

'A web of invisibility. Anything it touched would be rendered unseen…'

As Fatima gave voice to her fear, she took the cap from little Hashim's hand and pulled it down over her own head.

Instantly, she vanished.

Within a minute or two, Fatima and each of her children had tried on the cap. The youngest of the daughters was pulling the cap from her head when the father of the house came home. He asked to know the reason for such high excitement.

'A miracle, Baba!' Leila cried.

'Miracle?! What miracle?!'

'A magic cap… the one mother has knitted for you.'

Speaking all at once, the children described what had happened. And when they were silent, Fatima gave her own explanation about the spider of which her grandmother had spoken.

The woodcutter's daughters were jumping up and down, each of them begging to have another chance to experience the cap of invisibility. Clapping his hands together in anger, their father ordered them to quieten down.

'Leila!' the woodcutter growled. 'You are to take that cap to the river and throw it in!'

Fearful at igniting their father's rage, the four children agreed.

'Do as your father asks after you have done your homework, children,' the mother said.

'But Mother, I don't have any homework tonight,' Leila answered. 'So I will take the wool down to the river and throw it in.'

Taking the cap in her hand, Leila went out of the house and made her way to the river.

As she strode through the forest, she turned the situation around in her mind.

'If I do as my father says,' she thought to herself, 'the magic of the cap of invisibility will be lost. And, if that happens, it will never be available to be used in times of need. Although there's no way we know what may happen to us in the future, it's surely sensible to hide the cap of invisibility, so that it's available.'

Leila was an obedient girl but, in her eyes, good sense outweighed obedience.

Accordingly, she wrapped the cap of invisibility in her shawl, and stuffed it in a hollow in a blasted mulberry tree in the forest. Telling no one of what she had done, she returned home.

To her surprise, neither of her parents, nor her siblings, mentioned the magic cap of invisibility again.

Days, weeks, and months passed.

Then half a year.

Leila forgot about hiding the magic cap. It was as though the curious episode had never taken place.

One afternoon, while chopping wood, her father discovered a hoard of ancient gold coins hidden at the base of a tree he was cutting down. He was sitting on the ground, hands filled with glinting coins, when a pair of soldiers from the royal guard approached.

Being honest to the core, the woodcutter showed the coins to the soldiers and explained that he had just found them.

Certain no one would be so honest as to admit finding the coins, the soldiers assumed the woodcutter was only showing them a small fraction of a far larger treasure.

Drawing their swords, they threatened him.

'Reveal the entire hoard you have found, you wretched man,' one of them cried out, 'or we shall have you imprisoned in the deepest dungeon!'

Begging to be believed, the woodcutter invited the soldiers to take what he had found.

'I promise that I found no more of these,' he insisted. 'I am a simple man. And, although a treasure such as this would make a great difference to my existence, it is not my money to take.'

Making good on their threats, the officers of the royal guard put the woodcutter in chains and dragged him off to the dungeons.

Days passed before word of what had happened reached the ears of the woodcutter's family.

Distraught at the thought of her husband languishing in a cell, Fatima gathered her children all around her and told them to have faith in the divine.

That night, all four children and their mother prayed for their father, and went to bed.

But Leila was unable to sleep.

Lying on her back, she kept thinking that there must be a way to save her beloved father from the terrible cell in which he was imprisoned. As she lay there, she remembered the magic cap.

When she was sure all the others were fast asleep, Leila crept out of the house, paced through the forest, and made her way to the blasted mulberry tree.

To her delight, the magic cap was still there, wrapped in her shawl, just where she had left it months before.

Taking a deep breath, Leila pulled it on.

She didn't feel any different, and wondered whether it had lost its ability to make things invisible. But, putting her hand in front of her face in the moonlight, she couldn't see it. She was even invisible to herself.

With no plan to speak of, she hurried through the forest and then through the town, until she arrived at the palace walls. By this time, it was the middle of the night, and the streets were deserted.

A pair of low-ranking conscripts were standing guard at the gateway. Assuming they were alone, they were busily chatting to one another, telling jokes of the wise fool, Mulla Nasrudin.

Moving as fast as her feet could carry her, Leila hurried into the palace through a gap in the railings. She was going to try and locate the dungeons when something occurred to her… if she was to free her father, the entire family would be rounded up, and he himself would become a fugitive.

So, cautioning herself to think of a plan, she wandered the palace corridors, taking in the lavish surroundings.

Without meaning to trespass, she found herself in the queen's private chamber. The walls were hung with the finest textiles from the Orient, and the floors were laid in exquisite teak, with jewels inset.

In any other circumstances, Leila would have been more interested in the lavish décor, but all that was in her mind was saving her father.

Gliding through the private apartment in silence, the cap of invisibility pulled down tight, she heard the sound of a woman crying. Unable not to be intrigued, Leila paced through to a bedroom from where the sound was coming.

Before she knew it, she was standing in front of a grand bed, upon which the queen was sitting.

Head in hands, she was sobbing.

Having not come up with a plan, but being naturally curious, Leila whispered:

'Dearest queen, why do you weep?'

Startled at the sound of a child's voice, the queen looked up.

'Who's there?!'

'I am a good jinn,' Leila said. 'A good jinn who cares for your well-being.'

'But your voice is that of a child.'

'We jinn can take any form, as you know,' Leila said.

The queen nodded.

'I have heard as much. But pray tell, what can you do for me?'

'I will have to hear your predicament in full before I can give help.'

A moment later, the queen was mid-flow in a story of trial, tribulation, and woe. The tale explained why she was sobbing there on the edge of her bed in the middle of the night.

Despite endless twists, turns and all manner of complexities, her misery came down to a single fact... that she had been robbed a year before while out riding. While she was resting at the river's edge, a golden brooch had been stolen from her saddlebag by a fisherman.

She had learned of the theft from the kingdom's network of spies. Being a good queen, she didn't want to incriminate the fisherman. But day after day, the king asked what she had done with the golden brooch.

Once Leila had heard the tale, she thought long and hard.

And as first light broke across the horizon, she said:

'In order to regain the brooch, you will need to arrange for a humble woodcutter to be released from the prison beneath this very palace, to be pardoned, and to be given the golden hoard he himself discovered. You will order him to go to the home of the fisherman and ask for the brooch. In return, the value of the brooch will be paid to the fisherman from the gold coins. Even though he had stolen, he will be thanked by the woodcutter for cooperating.'

'And what do you require from me, O jinn?'

Leila thought for a moment.

'As a selfless jinn, I need nothing for myself,' she said. 'Instead, I ask that once each year, the wives and children of all woodcutters are honoured in a banquet here at the palace.'

The queen nodded.

It being the nod of royalty, it was as good as any promise.

Before the sun had set on the kingdom, the woodcutter was released from the dungeons. Dressed in fine attire and presented with the golden hoard he had discovered, he was sent to the home of the fisherman. Once an appropriate explanation had been made, the fisherman was given the correct number of coins in exchange for the brooch, and that object was presented by the woodcutter to the hand of the queen.

Returned to his family, the woodcutter had no clear understanding of what had taken place.

Leila never explained her role in his release to anyone – not even when she, her siblings, and her mother were guests of honour at the annual banquet, as they always were.

As for the magic cap of invisibility, once the golden brooch had been returned and her father pardoned, Leila wrapped it back in her shawl, and took it back to the hollow in the blasted mulberry tree…

…where it is waiting for you to find it and set out with it on a new adventure.

Only the Painting Knows the Whole Story

Ken & Duke Tate

THE DROP CLOTH was first aware of her existence, her essence, in a dark room with many people. Sunlight entered through the openings, and the drop cloth became ever more conscious of herself as the men and women handled her.

A child with a sweet aura and a happy smile, whose father owned the drop cloth factory, selected her from a staggering pile of other cloths. She was proud to be selected and felt the warmth of the sun through the skylight when she was unfolded and laid out on an old, hand- carved wooden table. She heard voices and was comforted by the vibration of the place and the people therein.

The drop cloth was then sewn onto another cloth like herself. Merging with the other cloth, the two became one.

The drop cloth liked her new size. She had more surface awareness. And she now realized that she was made of a heavy fabric. She liked the way she felt to herself.

She wanted to be of use somehow, and wondered why she had been created in the first place.

The drop cloth was then handled by more humans as they, carefully and with great skill, stitched her edges. The sewing made her feel defined and limited. Suddenly, her thoughts and feelings became more concentrated and focused. Before the edges had been stitched, she had felt free. Now she had a purpose, but she didn't quite know what it was.

She would have to wait to find out.

Sometimes, when she was still, she had the awareness of being a fluffy white cotton ball on a green stem in a field of other white balls, basking in the sunlight. Yes, those were the days. Things were simpler then, but she sensed a new journey lay ahead of her where she would aspire to be something more.

The drop cloth felt alive again, as if awakened from a deep sleep, when she was taken from her shelf and placed in a bag. Seeing through the bag, she felt herself being carried and then placed with other drop cloths onto rolling carts and then into big vans. Then, it was pitch black again.

The drop cloth felt the vibrations of the movement of the van and found pleasure in them. The spirit of adventure filled the drop cloth with joy, and she wondered if maybe, one day, she would wrap and comfort something wherever she was going – perhaps the people that had cared for her thus far? Although she didn't yet know it, she sensed she had been created for some magical purpose.

The drop cloth became fond of her existence travelling in the van. When the vehicle finally stopped moving, many people appeared and started touching and moving her and the other cloths.

The drop cloth was taken into a room with strong light. There were people in the room moving objects around from one cold, hard shelf to another. They were vibrating, but not as strongly as the ones before.

Then, one day, the drop cloth was taken from her cold spot on the shelf to another room. This room felt expansive, and people there were excited and playful. It was warmer, too. The drop cloth was proudly placed for all the store's customers to see, touch and handle. It felt so good to be around people again, and in her heart, she now loved them and somehow wanted to be of service to them.

Shortly after being placed on the shelf, the drop cloth was enthusiastically grabbed by an eccentric, curious little Italian man with Groucho Marx whiskers and a big nose with long, gnarly grey hairs. He wore a plaid newsboy hat and paint-splattered white canvas overalls. Seeing the outfit, the drop cloth thought, 'He has a canvas body just like me!' and giggled.

The man took her and placed her in a cart with other objects from the bright room and carried them to a register where he paid for her and the other things. Money was being exchanged and the drop cloth watched, pleased and curious. After being bought by the interesting man, the drop cloth had a little more self-awareness.

When the Groucho man took her into his studio, she sensed this was her special place – a place she could possibly serve people. However, when the man dropped her on the cold, hard floor, she began to worry. First of all, she got stepped on right away. It didn't hurt, but life was hard on the stone floor.

Nevertheless, the drop cloth became accustomed to her life under the Italian's feet. Through hearing conversations, she learned the painter's name was Tino and that their home was in California. He had a good vibe and radiated that onto her surface. One day, the drop cloth was moved into an important position where the man spent most of his time; she was still on the floor, but better somehow.

She started to feel some kind of wetness hit her surface. She had grown to know that this wetness had something important to do with the art Tino was always creating on the easel.

Although she was on the floor, the drop cloth had begun to like being there because she was performing a higher function than she had previously. At times, she thought, this was the reason she had been created – to serve – while at other times, she longed to be a painting on Tino's easel. As time passed, the drop cloth developed a deep thirst to be on the artist's easel like those other canvases, where she could be transformed by the artist into something greater.

Any day, she thought.

Over many months, while the drop cloth kept wishing to be a painting, the wet patterns on her surface started to make pictures like the ones on the easel. Not exactly the same – they were different, but better in an interesting way.

The drop cloth was aware of these patterns and could sense them like continents on a map of the world. Her surface started to know things, and to understand the meaning in the various shapes. This awareness gave the drop cloth feelings of sublime joy – her surface started to tingle, and she could feel the fibres of woven cotton rise and vibrate – ever so slightly, but still, they were rising as though stirred by the wind that once blew them in the field.

She knew that she had now finally discovered her purpose: to be a work of art. The drop cloth wanted to be a real piece of art so strongly that she gave all her energy to this one singular intention.

She willed the painter to notice one day how beautiful her art had already become, but he never seemed to look down.

The drop cloth continued her way with the paint, to receive and hold the drops that fell upon her surface, doing her best always to be a painting.

And, one day, the impossible happened quite accidentally: Tino dropped his brush onto the drop cloth, and when he reached down to get it, his muddy eyes widened and a smile emerged from behind his Groucho moustache. Like a crazed madman, he moved everything hurriedly off the cloth, and, lifting her up, attached her to the far wall so he could get a better look at her. There, Tino stood back, combed his moustache and kissed his fingertips, hollering, '*Che bello!*'

After that, he stood there like a Roman statue for hours, just peering into the mystery that had unfolded before his sleepy eyes.

Then, when he had taken in all of her beauty, he put the drop cloth back on the floor.

'Oh no,' thought the drop cloth, 'Tino's not going to put me on the easel where I belong.'

But lo and behold, Tino proceeded to get on his knees next to the drop cloth and speak to her gently, as if in a whisper, while caressing her surface with his paint-caked fingers.

'You are now one of my paintings. I don't know how this happened, but you have become one of my brightest creations. Perhaps it's because I didn't have to do anything, it just happened. All we did was *to allow*.'

And then, Tino went over to his work bench and carried his cradle of paints and brushes back to her. He made some intentional strokes here and there on her beautiful surface to even her out.

And in this way... the artist and his creation became one.

When Tino had finished, the drop cloth was even more sublime, returning to a state of joy at arriving at her destination. For the first time in her life, she was at peace.

As the days moved on, the drop cloth began to be admired by Tino's friends in the studio. He showed her to absolutely everyone in their little town, and through the paint on her surface, the colour and shapes, she told her story to them like the Arabian story of the camel that was turned into a storyteller and asked to tell his story to the world. In contrast to the camel, the drop cloth's vehicle was paint and cotton, rather than air and words, but the artist's friends understood the meaning just as clearly. The painting stayed with people, for it was glorious, and they would think about its meaning and its humble beginnings from time to time.

But even now, with all the admiration she enjoyed, the drop cloth was uneasy just hanging on the lonely wall. She needed something more to do, some greater purpose. First of all, she must be stretched onto a canvas like the other paintings she had seen, which then left the studio and went away. Where would she go next?

As days turned to months and months to years, she forgot about her longing and challenged herself to become content enough. It was true, she had a pretty good life with Tino and his friends there in the studio. They listened to music like Muddy Waters and Bob Dylan, and for a time she was able to forget her dream. But one day, Tino stopped coming to the studio, and the drop cloth fell into a deep depression. There was no sign of him for weeks.

Then, one night, rain fell from the sky so hard that the water rose in the streets around the studio by half a foot. Lightning flashed from the rolling black clouds and thunder banged outside the studio's windows. The light was off in her room, and all the cloth could hear was the roof-rattling booms in the distance. Now, all alone, the drop cloth thought to herself, '*Is this all there is?* I am a work of art, but I am still not happy.' With tears in her eyes, she dozed off.

In her sleep, she dreamed of children playing in the sun in the beautiful lush valleys of an imaginary kingdom blessed with never-ending peace. And she, the drop cloth, was somehow connected to it in a small but important way – she didn't quite know how or why, but it felt so good to be a thread in that rope and she was warm again.

The light flipped on in the studio, waking her. Tino came in. She observed that the rain had stopped outside as he walked over to her and took her gently off the wall. She was happy when she saw him, for in her heart, she had missed him deeply. As he folded her up, she wondered where they might be going.

Tino carried her into the kitchen of the main house, where his wife Maria was chopping onions. He explained that the wonderful painting had just been sold to the highest bidder at a charitable auction for children in great need, and would be travelling soon by mail to its new owner.

Hearing this, the painting knew her time had come to serve again, but this time, in a greater way than before. She felt happy and at ease. She felt complete.

The next day, Tino placed her in a package at the post office where she learned she now had a name: 'Only the Painting Knows the Whole Story'. She loved it, for she *was* her story and she was looking forward to sharing her journey from cotton ball to lowly drop cloth to painting to helping the world with everyone. While travelling, she thought, 'Everything has a myth and a purpose, telling your story to the world, whether you are an iguana or a "Get Lost in Idaho" cup or even a painting like I am, will be one of the most important things you do in your life.'

On Backgammon Time

Tahir Shah

I IMAGINE THAT the title of this tale means nothing to you.

After all, how could you have heard of such a curious thing?

There was a time when I was as you are now, unknowing and raw...

...a time when I had not ventured to the Land of Grosticam.

On another evening I will regale you with tales of my wider adventure, and explain how the curse that now afflicts me was meted out there.

But, for now, I would like to offer an episode that was quite unlike anything that had occurred in my life until that time.

It centred around my love for backgammon.

You see, I come from a family of traders... the kind who spend their lives in the old cities of the East. They while away the hours, waiting for buyers to peruse their wares. But such is life, and customers are few and far between. And that means one thing: a life of sweet mint tea, stories, and endless games of backgammon.

When youth had drained away into adulthood, my father pointed at me, then at the horizon.

'You are to go on a journey,' he said.

'Why, Baba?' I answered.

'Because you are far too clean and comfortable, and because if you are to succeed in life you will need hands far less smooth than you now have.'

'Where should I go?' I asked.

My father balked at the question.

'Anywhere… but only come back when what you take for certainty has been changed by experience.'

At dawn the next morning I set off and, after a litany of adventures, reached the ancient crumbling walls of that desert outpost – the Land of Grosticam.

At first glance there was nothing especially unusual about it. The buildings were made from stone hewn from the nearby mountains, which circled the plain. The bazaar was packed with the kind of wares found in such places, drawn from all corners of the compass.

There were heaps of ripe pomegranates and melons as fine as any I'd ever seen, baskets woven by prisoners in the next kingdom, and all manner of magical supplies, including blocks of sulphur and antimony.

Above the great bazaar, perched atop the city wall, was a teahouse.

By day and by night, a riotous miscellany of characters dwelt there, as though washed up by a freak wave of adventure. Most of them appeared to be fugitives, thieves, or liars. I was very careful not to have anything to do with any of them. But something stirred in me. It seemed as if I might at last be nearing the answer to the riddle my father had set me.

The day after my arrival, I noticed a very elderly man seated alone in the corner of the teahouse. He had wizened features, but a distinguished countenance. It appeared that he had been born of good blood but had fallen on hard times.

His only possession was a magnificent backgammon set.

To my surprise, no one ever challenged him to a game.

It being such an exquisite board, inlaid with mother of pearl, that I went over and introduced myself. The next thing I knew, I was seated across from the man, a shaker in my hand.

Before rolling to ascertain who was to take black and who was to take white, I asked whether we were playing for money. For, even in the bazaars of my own land, the merchants wagered a small amount so as to make it a little more exciting.

The wizened owner of the backgammon set ran the side of his hand down his long nose, like a bird preening a wing.

'In Grosticam we do not play for coinage,' he answered. 'Rather, we play for a different kind of currency.'

I frowned, then managed half a smile.

'I don't understand,' I said.

The ancient sniffed hard, his nostrils distending.

'We play for time,' he said.

I did not understand. But, imbued with youthful enthusiasm, I shrugged.

'Sounds as fine a currency as any to me,' I riposted.

And with that, I shook the dice, and so did he.

A youth spent in the bazaars of my own country had, I mused, afforded me a clear advantage. For, right from the start, I dominated.

The game was going so well for me that at one stage I even apologized.

My wizened opponent said nothing; he simply smiled wryly to himself.

A little time after the first game had begun, my run of luck with the dice turned. It was as though they were against me. However devious my play, I didn't get the numbers I needed.

And to my despair, the first game went to him.

As I bemoaned my loss, slapping a hand playfully to my knee, something happened that took me by surprise… something that caused me to shake right down to the bone.

You see, as I conceded defeat, I felt myself age by a decade. And, at the same moment, my wizened challenger appeared ten years younger than he had moments before.

I frowned and cursed.

He smiled.

'What just happened?' I asked quickly.

'Time,' uttered my opponent.

'You mean…?'

'Time slipped away from you and came to me.'

I swallowed hard.

'But how could such a monstrous thing take place?!'

The man across from me smiled again. His skin was brighter, his eyes less sagged.

'By the magic of the board,' he said.

'You mean that ten years of my life have been stolen from me?!' I cried.

'No, no,' the player corrected, 'they have not been stolen from you. They have been *won* from you.'

I sat there, perspiration running down my face as my mind turned in horror.

What was I to do…?

Play on, and risk losing more time while rejuvenating my adversary?

…Or leave now and return home older and more ripened than I would have wished?

Chilled with fear, I agreed to a second game. I would stop at nothing until I had defeated him, drawing on the tactics I'd seen used in the bazaars of my home town.

So, we played a second game.

This time, he went first, and got a streak of good dice.

But then, as so often happens, the numbers changed in my favour.

I was drenched in sweat, but my opponent was calm as calm could be. I found this remarkable, as though he were unfazed by the thought of losing his recent gains.

The game went on and on, each one of us playing more brilliantly than I have ever seen on a board so lovely as that one.

The ancient, who of course was no longer quite so aged, had a mastery that impressed me greatly.

But as we reached the end of the match, it was I who trounced him.

'*Hah!*' I exclaimed in the most spirited voice ever to have left my lungs.

As the sound drifted out through the open window and over the old city of Grosticam, I felt the lost decade return.

At the same time, my adversary's appearance was as aged as it had been when I first challenged him.

As soon as the second game was over, I shook his hand and expressed my sincerest thanks for the most enlivening and dangerous of afternoons.

'I do not wish to appear impolite,' I said, 'but, after all, an elderly gentleman such as yourself has already enjoyed a long life and, I hope, a happy one.'

The man looked at me, his eyes glazed over with cataracts.

A single tear welled in his left eye and ran down the length of his cheek, the skin of his face wrinkled like elephant hide.

'Might I enquire your age?' he said.

I told him.

'I'm twenty.'

The ancient sniffed again, as though greatly troubled.

'I am the same age as you,' he said.

My gaze roamed from his face down onto the board, that damned backgammon board, the one that controlled the currency of life and death.

'I am *so* sorry,' I whispered.

And with that, I left the teahouse, my head hung low in gratitude and in shame.

Returning to my father's mountainside, I spoke the story of Grosticam.

When the last word had left my mouth, I said:

'Baba, when I embarked from this hillside, I believed that a day lived was a day imprinted onto my soul. But now that I have experienced that wretched board, I can never again take time for granted. After all, whatever we believe it to be, time is quite evidently not what it would seem.'

Nasrudin: Camouflage

Tahir Shah

ALTHOUGH DOING HIS best to blend in with local culture, Nasrudin managed to offend one of the most powerful Triad families in China.

Terrified out of his wits, he spent weeks hiding from the gang members.

But whenever he slipped out of his hiding place to buy food, he would spot more of them – each one dressed in baggy black clothes, every inch of their skin tattooed.

Suddenly, an idea slipped onto the stage of his mind.

He bought a black outfit and hurried into the tattoo parlour across the street.

'What would you like tattooed?' the artist asked, taking in the unlikely customer.

Nasrudin glanced at the walls, which were covered with Triad tattoos.

He pointed to the most elaborate full-body tattoo he could see.

'That,' he said.

As he prepared his equipment and the inks, the artist cocked his head at the picture on the walls.

'If you don't mind me asking, why would a man like you want a Triad tattoo like that?'

Nasrudin smiled wryly as though he were about to outwit his pursuers.

'Camouflage,' he said.

The Wondrous Seed

Tahir Shah

ONCE UPON A time, before the great continents had risen from the seas, there was an island known by its inhabitants as Pop-tica-pie.

Little more than a tiny speck of dry land in an endless expanse of blue, it was a paradise. The people who lived there had no contact with anyone else, but they were the happiest folk you could ever hope to meet. They spent their days in the forest, down at the water's edge, or at the ancient altar which was in between the two.

The people of Pop-tica-pie sang and laughed all day long, and when they slept, they smiled. No one there ever wondered whether they were the happiest people in all the world, because they assumed they were the *only* people in existence.

Once in a while, what looked like an object would be seen far in the distance, the size of a pea running the length of the horizon. When such an object was spotted, the people would gather at the great altar and sing a song in honour of the ancestors for revealing a little magic to amuse them.

No one on the island went without food or fresh water. They fashioned themselves clothing from the fibres of palm fronds and, when the summer storms raged, they would cluster together at the altar, singing a song of wonder and woe.

On a day much like any other, a little boy called Salap went down to the water's edge to search for shells. He was kind, thoughtful, and the apple of his parents' eye. If there was anything that singled him out from the other boys, it was his inquisitive nature.

So, Salap was paddling in the water looking for shells, when he spotted something bobbing up and down. Curious as to what it might be, he waded out, grabbed the object, and hurried back to the beach.

Squatting on the sand, Salap examined it.

It was unlike anything he had ever seen before. As wide as his torso, it was wooden, curved, and quite alluring.

Unsure what to do, Salap carried it up the beach and to the home where he lived with his parents in the shade of the great palm tree.

Within ten minutes, a crowd had gathered, everyone wishing to see the peculiar object that little Salap had found. One at a time, they leaned forward and touched it, laughing and singing with delight.

'It was sent to us by the ancestors as a musical instrument. Listen how it rattles when it's shaken!' an old woman cried out.

'It is a float to use in fishing!' yelled someone else.

'No, no,' corrected a third, 'it's a throne on which the leader of the island must sit!'

All day, the people of Pop-tica-pie chattered, laughed, and sang about the object that Salap had discovered in the sea. And all night long, each one of them imagined what they would use it for.

The morning after the curious object had been discovered, the man who had assumed it was a float grabbed it and ran out into the water with it to show the others. The ancient who had thought it was an instrument yelled out that the fisherman had stolen it. Then, the man who thought it was a throne snatched it away from the fisherman. Positioning it close to the altar, he sat down on it, and sang triumphantly.

By nightfall, the harmony of the island was lost.

Everyone, from the smallest child to the oldest and most wizened crone, wanted to have their time with the object. Accordingly, a rota system was drawn up, in which everyone – irrespective of gender or age – was permitted a few minutes with the object. But despite good intentions, the system caused infighting and hostility right from the start.

Everyone, it seemed, accused everyone else of taking too long when it was their turn. As the days of the rota progressed, the people of Pop-tica-pie began treating the object too roughly. One of the little boys dropped it against a rock, and the outer covering of fibrous husk fell away.

All the people came together in sorrow.

For the first time in as long as anyone could remember, the laughter and the singing ceased.

The people of the island were truly sad that their beloved object, the one thing which had brought universal delight and joy, was damaged.

Calling everyone to the altar, the leader of the community ordered that they would do what they always did in times of uncertainty.

They would ask the ancestors what to do.

And so, as the sun slipped down below the horizon and dusk fell, every mouth whispered a plea to the ancestors, asking what to do with the magical object from the sea.

All night, the people of Pop-tica-pie whispered...

...and all the next day...

...and through the next night...

Then, as dawn broke over the horizon, something happened which was witnessed by everyone.

A little mouse burrowed up out of the sand and scampered into the undergrowth beyond the beach.

His lungs filling with air, the head of the community cried out:

'See that – a sign! See the sign sent by the ancestors!'

'What does it mean we should do?' asked the oldest crone.

'It means we must bury the object in the ground,' said Salap, the boy who had discovered it in the first place. 'Because if it is buried, then no one can damage it, and it can continue towards its own destiny.'

Every man, woman, and child spoke at once – quizzing, questioning, cooing, and demanding.

As their noise grew louder than anything the island had ever experienced, the head man raised a hand in the air.

'Salap was the person who found the object,' he said. 'So, it should be Salap who decides. If he thinks the mouse was a sign that we must bury the object sent by the ancestors, then that is what we shall do!'

A spade was brought out, and a spot at the edge of the forest was chosen.

With everyone crowding around, Salap dug a hole and placed the object into it. Before it was covered up with soil, each member of the community was allowed to reach forwards and touch it one last time.

Weeks passed.

Then, months.

After almost a year, Salap was wandering up from the beach with some shells he had found, when he spotted something at the edge of the forest... something that had not been there before.

A little green shoot...

...a little green shoot growing straight up.

Calling out as loudly as he could, Salap announced what he had seen.

Instantly, everyone clustered around.

The oldest crone rubbed a thumb to each eye and gasped.

'It was a seed!' she exclaimed.

'A seed sent by the ancestors!' the others sang.

Many more months passed.

The shoot grew and grew...

...and grew and grew...

Up... up... up...

And as it grew, the people of Pop-tica-pie would cluster around and sing songs to the plant, or rather, the tree.

Because that's what the seed had grown into – a magnificent palm, unlike any other on the island.

On some nights when the summer storms raged and the people clustered together to sing, they would take it in turns to remember the time when the mysterious object was found by the little boy, Salap – the little boy who was now a grown man.

They would remember how they all fought because they loved the object, and because they wanted to make use of it. And they would remember that only by planting did they come to realize it was in actual fact a seed... a seed that, by growing into a tree, could be loved and celebrated by all.

Many more years passed.

Eventually, Salap had great-grandchildren.

One afternoon, as they waded through the shallows in search of shells, one of them called out on their way back from the sea.

'Look! Look!' she called.

All the people of Pop-tica-pie clustered around.

'What's wrong?'

'Look up at the magical tree... the one which you all talk about all the time!'

Every face looked up at the tree.

Then, every mouth gasped.

You see, high above the tree's trunk were a clutch of coconuts growing, just like the one Salap had found as a boy.

With time, the coconuts grew to maturity and they were planted in the forest, so that they could reach their destiny and cause no jealousy.

And when those seeds grew into palms and had coconuts of their own, some were planted, and others were taken into the waves and released…

So that they could travel over oceans, and give joy to others across the seas.

The Paradise Tree

Tahir Shah

ONCE UPON A time, a young man from a distant kingdom arrived at the great bazaar of Samarkand.

His name was Karim, and he was descended from a long line of carpet weavers. From the earliest days of childhood, the children of his family were encouraged to imagine fabulous new patterns which, with time, they would be able to weave into the carpets they conjured in their workshop at the foot of the great mountains.

With each day that passed, Karim had been evermore enthused at starting work as a weaver. But when his studies were finished, his father had called Karim to attend him.

'Are you ready to start your career as a weaver,' he had asked, 'and to weave carpets as your ancestors have done?'

Straightening his back with pride, the youth had nodded.

'Yes, Father. I am ready.'

'Well, before you can start, you must go on a journey and search for something that has no value, but which is valued more than anything else known to man.'

Although piqued at being sent on what he assumed to be a deviation from a life at the loom, Karim set off on a journey, and that is how he came to find himself in the great bazaar at Samarkand.

With no money to his name, the young man set about doing odd jobs to earn enough to buy a kebab at one of the low stalls at the edge of the market. By the end of the afternoon, he had made three or four brass coins – enough for a single skewer of meat.

Handing the money over, he took a kebab in exchange and went over to the shadow of a wall, where various impoverished people were sitting about.

Karim was just about to swallow the first cube of succulent meat when he saw an exceptionally ragged dervish looking at him. He appeared famished, as though he hadn't eaten in days.

Pausing, the youth lowered the kebab from his mouth and offered it to the man. Giving thanks, the wizened old dervish took the kebab and devoured it.

Hunger gnawing at his ribs, Karim smiled at the dervish.

'*Thank you*, O Baba, for allowing me to help you in your moment of need,' he said.

The dervish smiled.

'Judging by your attire you are, like me, from a faraway land,' he said. 'From a place where people have very good manners. In the place where I am from there are two traditions we live by. The first is to feed someone more hungry than oneself, which you have done. The second tradition is that we always return a favour.'

Karim held up a hand.

'Please, Baba, there is no reason to bless me with any favour in return. After all, your need is clearly greater than mine.'

The wizened old dervish held out a palm to silence the young man. Then, his hands shaking with age, he fumbled with something tied around his neck.

A moment later, he had removed what looked in the lengthening shadows like an amulet... the size and shape of an almond.

'This is for you,' the dervish said.

'What is it?'

'An object of destiny.'

'A talisman?'

The dervish shook his head.

'It's a seed,' he said.

Karim gave thanks, then asked what he was supposed to do with it.

'Plant it,' answered the ancient.

'Plant it... *where*?'

'On the top of a mountain.'

Not wishing to appear ungrateful, Karim might have asked why he would need to plant the seed, or indeed what species of flora it came from. But his father had always told him to be a man of action rather than of questions.

So, next morning, he left Samarkand – the seed in his pocket, his gaze on the mountains at the horizon.

Days of climbing and nights of freezing passed.

Then, after much hardship, Karim reached the apex of the highest mountain.

The ground was frozen and all covered in snow. And he was far too high for any vegetation to grow.

But, doing as instructed to do, he managed to clear the snow and ice from a little space and plant the seed.

Karim was about to turn on his heel and make his way back down the mountain when he sensed what seemed like the tremoring of an earthquake. Terrified, he fell to the ground and held onto a snow-covered rock.

To his astonishment, the mountain was shaking as a result of the seed growing.

As the youth watched, the tiny object let out a bright red shoot, replete with leaves and berries. And it shot straight up into the cobalt-blue sky.

Five minutes later, an immense tree was standing in the exact same spot where he had planted the dervish's seed. The trunk was mottled and grey, as though weathered and worn by the elements for centuries, and the boughs reached out in all directions.

Frozen to the bone, Karim wondered what to do. Just then, he spotted footholds carved into the side of the tree in a crude kind of ladder.

Not giving it any further thought, he strode up to the tree and began to climb.

He climbed and he climbed, and he climbed and he climbed.

Rather than getting colder as he ascended, Karim realized it was getting warmer.

But that wasn't what intrigued him.

You see, the higher he climbed, the more riotously his mind raced, as if it was being fed with nutrients of some magical and amazing variety.

All of a sudden, he could think up answers to every problem that had ever bewildered him. Without trying, his mind was spewing out poetry and music, and he felt his entire body tingling as it had never tingled before.

Delighted and confused, Karim whispered thanks to the dervish, and then thanked his own parents for bringing him up to be well mannered. After all, his good manners had led directly to the experience.

Then, just as he was about to peer down through the branches to the plains far below, he heard a voice.

'Follow me,' it said.

Squinting, Karim put a hand to his face.

'I can't see you... who is there?'

'No one is there... or rather *here*,' said the voice. 'It is I who is speaking.'

'*I*? Who?'

'I am the tree.'

'Since when could trees speak?' asked Karim.

The tree let out a gruff chuckle.

'I am the Paradise Tree, so of course I can speak,' it replied.

The youth took a deep breath. Before he could exhale, he had been cocooned in twigs and was being carried along to the very top of the tree. As if in a dream, he had no fear or sense of trepidation.

Instead, he marvelled at the experience.

And as he marvelled, he set eyes on what looked like a plain wooden door framed against one of the boughs. Before he knew it, the door had opened and he had been ferried inside by the tree itself.

Inside was not a room as he had expected, but a kingdom.

...A vast, magical, quixotic and illuminating kingdom.

As Karim's mind raced, he heard a voice... the voice of the tree...

'*This* is Paradise,' it said with slow perfection.

'Has my time on the earth come to an end,' Karim asked, 'that I am being spirited away here?'

'I said it was Paradise, not heaven,' the tree riposted. 'The two are not necessarily one and the same.'

'So, what is the need for this Paradise? Or, rather, I should ask why you have brought me here?'

'You are here,' the Paradise Tree explained, 'because of the reason you set out from your father's workshop all those weeks and months ago.'

Karim thought for a moment.

'I have been sent to search for something that has no value, but which is valued more than anything else known to man,' he said.

'Precisely,' the tree answered. 'Now, take your time and explore this kingdom.'

'You mean, explore *Paradise*?'

'Yes, explore Paradise,' said the tree, 'and when you have seen enough, come to me and tell me what you think.'

So, following orders once again, Karim, the son of the weaver, roamed Paradise far and wide. He encountered blissful landscapes – wilderness, forests, mountains, and even deserts – all of them utterly perfect. He met people kinder and more enlightened than any he had ever known, visited magnificent cities, and glimpsed the most glorious expressions of beauty imaginable.

Then, one morning, he awoke on the edge of a forest and sensed himself pining for home.

'O Paradise Tree,' he thought to himself, 'this is more wondrous than I can describe, but I am ready to be back in the imperfect world that I know and love.'

A blinding flash of light came and went.

Karim found himself sitting beside the hearth of his family home, his father beside him.

'Have you discovered something that has no value, but which is valued more than anything else known to man?'

The youth looked into his father's eyes and smiled.

'I have, Baba,' he answered. 'It's called the Paradise Tree.'

This story may well strike you as a fiction, to amuse a child before bed.

But turn it around your mind, allow it to live inside you, and year on year it will provide nourishment…

… just as the fruits of a tree nourish us yesterday, today, and will do so for a thousand more tomorrows.

The Islanders

Idries Shah

ONCE UPON A time, there lived an ideal community in a far-off land. Its members had no fears as we now know them. Instead of uncertainty and vacillation, they had purposefulness and a fuller means of expressing themselves.

Although there were none of the stresses and tensions which mankind now considers essential to its progress, their lives were richer, because other, better elements replaced these things. Theirs, therefore, was a slightly different mode of existence. We could almost say that our present perceptions are a crude, makeshift version of the real ones which this community possessed.

They had real lives, not semi-lives.

We can call them the El Ar people.

They had a leader, who discovered that their country was to become uninhabitable for a period of, shall we say, twenty thousand years. He planned their escape, realizing that their descendants would be able to return home successfully, only after many trials.

He found for them a place of refuge, an island whose features were only roughly similar to those of the original homeland. Because of the difference in climate and situation, the immigrants had to undergo a transformation. This made them more physically and mentally adapted to the new circumstances; coarse perceptions, for instance, were substituted for finer ones, as when the hand of the manual labourer becomes toughened in response to the needs of his calling.

In order to reduce the pain which a comparison between the old and new states would bring, they were made to forget the past almost entirely. Only the most shadowy recollection of it remained, yet it was sufficient to be awakened when the time came.

The system was very complicated, but well arranged. The organs by means of which the people survived on the island were also made the organs of enjoyment, physical and mental. The organs which were really constructive in the old homeland were placed in a special form of abeyance, and linked with the shadowy memory, in preparation for its eventual activation.

Slowly and painfully the immigrants settled down, adjusting themselves to the local conditions. The resources of the island were such that, coupled with effort and a certain form of guidance, people would be able to escape to a further island, on the way back to their original home. This was the first of a succession of islands upon which gradual acclimatization took place.

The responsibility of this 'evolution' was vested in those individuals who could sustain it. These were necessarily only a few, be cause for the mass of the people the effort of keeping both sets of knowledge in their consciousness was virtually impossible. One of them seemed to conflict with the other one. Certain specialists guarded the 'special science'.

This 'secret', the method of effecting the transition, was nothing more or less than the knowledge of maritime skills and their application. The escape needed an instructor, raw materials, people, effort and understanding. Given these, people could learn to swim, and also to build ships.

The people who were originally in charge of the escape operations made it clear to everyone that a certain preparation was necessary before anyone could learn to swim or even take part in building a ship. For a time the process continued satisfactorily.

Then a man who had been found, for the time being, lacking in the necessary qualities rebelled against this order and managed to develop a masterly idea. He had observed that the effort to escape placed a heavy and often seemingly unwelcome burden upon the people. At the same time they were disposed to believe things which they were told about the escape operation. He realized that he could acquire power, and also revenge himself upon those who had undervalued him, as he thought, by a simple exploitation of these two sets of facts.

He would merely offer to take away the burden, by affirming that there was no burden.

He made this announcement:

'There is no need for man to integrate his mind and train it in the way which has been described to you. The human mind is already a stable and continuous, consistent thing. You have been told that you have to become a craftsman in order to build a ship. I say, not only do you not need to be a craftsman – you do not need a ship at all! An islander needs only to observe a few simple rules to survive and remain integrated into society. By the exercise of common sense, born into everyone, he can attain anything upon this island, our home, the common property and heritage of all!'

The tonguester, having gained a great deal of interest among the people, now 'proved' his message by saying:

'If there is any reality in ships and swimming, show us ships which have made the journey, and swimmers who have come back!'

This was a challenge to the instructors which they could not meet. It was based upon an assumption of which the bemused herd could not now see the fallacy. You see, ships never returned from the other land. Swimmers, when they did come back, had undergone a fresh adaptation which made them invisible to the crowd.

The mob pressed for demonstrative proof.

'Shipbuilding,' said the escapers, in an attempt to reason with the revolt, 'is an art and a craft. The learning and the exercise of this lore depends upon special techniques. These together make up a total activity, which cannot be examined piecemeal, as you demand. This activity has an impalpable element, called *baraka*, from which the word "barque" – a ship – is derived. This word means "the Subtlety", and it cannot be shown to you.'

'Art, craft, total, *baraka*, nonsense!' shouted the revolutionaries.

And so they hanged as many shipbuilding craftsmen as they could find.

The new gospel was welcomed on all sides as one of liberation. Man had discovered that he was already mature! He felt, for the time at least, as if he had been released from responsibility.

Most other ways of thinking were soon swamped by the simplicity and comfort of the revolutionary concept. Soon it was considered to be a basic fact which had never been challenged by any rational person. Rational, of course, meant anyone who harmonized with the general theory itself, upon which society was now based.

Ideas which opposed the new one were easily called irrational. Anything irrational was bad. Thereafter, even if he had doubts, the individual had to suppress them or divert them, because he must at all costs be thought rational.

It was not very difficult to be rational. One had only to adhere to the values of society. Further, evidence of the truth of rationality abounded – providing that one did not think beyond the life of the island.

Society had now temporarily equilibrated itself within the island, and seemed to provide a plausible completeness, if viewed by means of itself. It was based upon reason plus emotion, making both seem plausible. Cannibalism, for instance, was permitted on rational grounds. The human body was found to be edible. Edibility was a characteristic of food. Therefore the human body was food. In order to compensate for the shortcomings of this reasoning, a makeshift was arranged. Cannibalism was controlled, in the interests of society. Compromise was the trademark of temporary balance. Every now and again someone pointed out a new compromise, and the struggle between reason, ambition and community produced some fresh social norm.

Since the skills of boatbuilding had no obvious application within this society, the effort could easily be considered absurd. Boats were not needed – there was nowhere to go. The consequences of certain assumptions can be made to 'prove' those assumptions. This is what is called pseudo-certainty, the substitute for real certainty. It is what we deal in every day, when we assume that we will live another day.

But our islanders applied it to everything.

It is hardly surprising that from quite early times the very thought of leaving the island filled most people with terror. Similarly, very real fear is to be seen in long-term prisoners who are about to be released. 'Outside' the place of captivity is a vague, unknown, threatening world.

The island was not a prison. But it was a cage with invisible bars, more effective than obvious ones ever could be.

The insular society became more and more complex, and we can look at only a few of its outstanding features. Its literature was a rich one. In addition to cultural compositions there were numerous books which explained the values and achievements of the nation. There was also a system of allegorical fiction which portrayed how terrible life might have been, had society not arranged itself in the present reassuring pattern.

From time to time instructors tried to help the whole community to escape. Captains sacrificed themselves for the re-establishment of a climate in which the now concealed shipbuilders could continue their work. All these efforts were interpreted by historians and sociologists with reference to conditions on the island, without thought for any contact outside this closed society. Plausible explanations of almost anything were comparatively easy to produce. No principle of ethics was involved, because scholars continued to study with genuine dedication what seemed to be true. 'What *more* can we do?' they asked, implying by the word 'more' that the alternative might be an effort of quantity. Or they asked each other, 'What *else* can we do?' assuming that the answer might be in 'else' – something different. Their real problem was that they assumed themselves able to formulate the questions, and ignored the fact that the questions were every bit as important as the answers.

Of course the islanders had plenty of scope for thought and action within their own small domain. The variations of ideas and differences of opinion gave the impression of freedom of thought. Thought was encouraged, providing that it was not 'absurd'.

Freedom of speech was allowed. It was of little use without the development of understanding, which was not pursued.

The work and the emphasis of the navigators had to take on different aspects in accordance with the changes in the community. This made their reality even more baffling to the students who tried to follow them from the island point of view.

Amid all the confusion, even the capacity to remember the possibility of escape could at times become an obstacle. The stirring consciousness of escape potential was not very discriminating. More often than not the eager would-be escapers settled for any kind of substitute. A vague concept of navigation cannot become useful without orientation. Even the most eager potential shipbuilders had been trained to believe that they already had that orientation. They were already mature. They hated anyone who pointed out that they might need a preparation.

Bizarre versions of swimming or shipbuilding often crowded out possibilities of real progress. Very much to blame were the advocates of pseudo-swimming or allegorical ships, mere hucksters, who offered lessons to those as yet too weak to swim, or passages on ships which they could not build.

The needs of the society had originally made necessary certain forms of efficiency and thinking which developed into what was known as science. This admirable approach, so essential in the fields where it had an application, finally outran its real meaning. The approach called 'scientific', soon after the 'Please' revolution, became stretched until it covered all manner of ideas. Eventually things which could not be brought within its bounds became known as 'unscientific', another convenient synonym for 'bad'. Words were unknowingly taken prisoner and then automatically enslaved.

In the absence of a suitable attitude, like people who, thrown upon their own resources in a waiting room, feverishly read magazines, the islanders absorbed themselves in finding substitutes for the fulfilment which the original (and indeed the final) purpose of this community's exile.

Some were able to divert their attention more or less successfully into mainly emotional commitments. There were different ranges of emotion, but no adequate scale for measuring them. All emotion was considered to be 'deep' or 'profound' – at any rate more profound than non-emotion. Emotion, which was seen to move people to the most extreme physical and mental acts known, was automatically termed 'deep'.

The majority of people set themselves targets, or allowed others to set them for them. They might pursue one cult after another, or money, or social prominence. Some worshipped some things and felt themselves superior to all the rest. Some, by repudiating what they thought worship was, thought that they had no idols, and could therefore safely sneer at all the rest.

As the centuries passed, the island was littered with the debris of these cults. Worse than ordinary debris, it was self-perpetuating. Well-meaning and other people combined the cults and recombined them, and they spread anew. For the amateur and intellectual, this constituted a mine of academic or 'initiatory' material, giving a comforting sense of variety.

Magnificent facilities for the indulging of limited 'satisfactions' proliferated. Palaces and monuments, museums and universities, institutes of learning, theatres and sports stadiums almost filled the island. The people naturally prided themselves on these endowments, many of which they considered to be linked in a general way with ultimate truth, though exactly how this was so escaped almost all of them.

Shipbuilding was connected with some dimensions of this activity, but in a way unknown to almost everyone.

Clandestinely the ships raised their sails, the swimmers continued to teach swimming...

The conditions on the island did not entirely fill these dedicated people with dismay. After all, they too had originated in the very same community, and had indissoluble bonds with it, and with its destiny.

But they very often had to preserve themselves from the attentions of their fellow citizens. Some 'normal' islanders tried to save them from themselves. Others tried to kill them, for an equally sublime reason. Some even sought their help eagerly, but could not find them.

All these reactions to the existence of the swimmers were the result of the same cause, filtered through different kinds of minds. This cause was that hardly anyone now knew what a swimmer really was, what he was doing, or where he could be found.

As the life of the island became more and more civilized, a strange but logical industry grew up. It was devoted to ascribing doubts to the validity of the system under which society lived. It succeeded in absorbing doubts about social values by laughing at them or satirizing them. The activity could wear a sad or happy face, but it really became a repetitious ritual. A potentially valuable industry, it was often prevented from exercising its really creative function.

People felt that, having allowed their doubts to have temporary expression, they would in some way assuage them, exorcize them, almost propitiate them. Satire passed for meaningful allegory; allegory was accepted but not digested. Plays, books, films, poems, lampoons were the usual media for this development, though there was a strong section of it in more academic fields. For many islanders it seemed more emancipated, more modern or progressive, to follow this cult rather than older ones.

Here and there a candidate still presented himself to a swimming instructor, to make his bargain. Usually what amounted to a stereotyped conversation took place...

'I want to learn to swim.'

'Do you want to make a bargain about it?'

'No. I only have to take my ton of cabbage.'

'What cabbage?'

'The food which I will need on the other island.'

'There is better food there.'

'I don't know what you mean. I cannot be sure. I must take my cabbage.'

'You cannot swim, for one thing, with a ton of cabbage.'

'Then I cannot go. You call it a load. I call it my essential nutrition.'

'Suppose, as an allegory, we say not "cabbage", but "assumptions", or "destructive ideas"?'

'I am going to take my cabbage to some instructor who understands my needs.'

The fable is not ended, because there are still people on the island.

The Sufis use various ciphers to convey their meaning. Rearrange the name of the original community – El Ar – to spell 'Real'. Perhaps you had already noticed that the name adopted by the revolutionaries – 'Please' – rearranges to form the word 'Asleep'.

Very Slippy Weather

Jason Webster

Dear Mr. Gillray,

As you are currently away in the country, I wish to tell you about an amusing little incident which took place this morning outside the shop, an Event which, in my estimation, may provide sufficient material for a new caricature, not least because my shop, your caricatures and our esteemed mutual friend the Reverend Sneyd were all principal players in the comedy that unfolded. (I use the word 'comedy' advisedly, for the Reverend was very much the butt of the joke, and while his physical injuries are on the mend, those to his pride will take time to heal.)

This unusually cold weather we've been experiencing was the Prime Mover of the drama. Thanks to the recent legacy from his aunt (the details of which I have no need to bore you with not least because Sneyd himself has done a good enough job of that), the Reverend decided yesterday to purchase a new pair of boots, his old ones having become rather worn and leaky. Inspired by this new acquisition, he subsequently decided to spend more money on fixing his Thermometer, which, as you will also be aware, he was convinced had become faulty, refusing to reflect the 'true coldness' of the time of year. (Why he needs 'scientific' confirmation of what anyone can feel in their bones is beyond me. But I digress.)

So this morning, armed with the Thermometer, and suitably attired in his shiny new boots, he set forth for St. James's Street where, at No. 19, Mr. Jones the watchmaker is famed for his qualities as a repairer of all things mechanical.

Thus it was that the Reverend found himself walking past No. 27, my shop and your home, and it was here that Fate intervened. The slope of St. James's Street is not insignificant, and it would appear that the Reverend had made every effort to carry his beloved Thermometer with all due care and attention for, as he has repeated to me more than once since, the Mercury therein is its most precious commodity and the reason why such objects command the high prices that they do.

'A thermometer without its Mercury is like a man without his Soul: an empty shell without purpose in God's Creation.'

(One might be forgiven for imagining that the events I am about to relate, while possibly providing you with another caricature, will, in the Reverend's case, be transformed into a most lengthy and enlightening Sunday morning sermon.)

As he approached my establishment, the Reverend noticed that the usual crowd was gathered outside the window, gazing with amused intent at your wares displayed within each pane of glass, as per our custom. Labouring with his Thermometer, and less sure underfoot than he might have wished to be, the Reverend asked members of the public to clear a way for him that he might get past.

Some of them were known to him, indeed were quite intimate acquaintances, but, as though speaking to the deaf, his words failed to have the desired effect, for the spectators of your work were so fixated on the caricatures on display that it was as if they were unconcerned, indeed unaware, of all events around them. Drawing on his many years as a man of the cloth and thereby accustomed to addressing large congregations, the Reverend raised his voice and once again appealed for passage through the crowd. Yet again he was paid no heed.

Around this time, the Reverend Sneyd was beginning to entertain considerable doubts about the fine pair of boots of which he had availed himself only the day before. While his old ones had indeed been in a sorry state, yet their very roughness had made them more suited to the current icy and very slippy weather. By contrast, the new footwear gracing his lower limbs was as soft and smooth as the skin of a new-born babe. With some alarm, he began to understand that the combination of the ice underfoot, the downward slope and the difficulty of his movement through the crowd were about to place his precious cargo in grave danger, and so, with all the dignity he could muster, he made a Momentous Decision.

It was at this very moment that I, alerted by the sound of his voice, looked out from the upstairs window, from which vantage point I was able to witness the Event. Needless to say, it all took place in much less time than it takes to tell, indeed in the blinking of an eye, but as you yourself have commented, there are such moments, short in mere temporal duration, which, for reasons which cannot always be explained, nonetheless endure for a much greater time thereafter in the imagination, and I believe that this was just such a one.

As I watched, the Reverend made a tentative step forwards, as though through the power of movement alone he might convince the crowd (who still had no awareness of his presence, so enthralled were they with your work) that they might give way. Seeing that this failed to have the desired outcome, he then launched himself forwards, beating the paving stones with his cane as one who threshes wheat. At first this appeared to bring dividends, as he made some clear progress, taking two, three and even four strides forwards while the crowd, still unseeing, parted way for him, as though by Divine Intervention.

At this moment, one might be forgiven for imagining the Reverend's mind being populated with passages from Exodus referring to the Red Sea and its ability to part on command, yet if this was the case, he was about to be undone. Earlier that morning, long before dawn, young Sarah the housemaid had mopped the entrance to the shop and thrown out the waste water into the street. Yet, this being an unusually cold time of year, she had tossed the water not from the far side of the pavement, but from the very doorstep (for fear of catching a cold herself), with the result that not a small amount of it had fallen on the paving stones. It being dark at the time, no notice of it was made, and indeed the whole day might well have progressed without her act going detected in any way, but for the arrival several hours later of the Reverend Sneyd with his Thermometer and wearing his new boots.

So it was that, fired by his unexpected and quite miraculous sudden progress through the previously unmovable crowd, the Reverend strode swiftly and confidently across this particularly icy patch, which was where his spectacular fall from grace occurred. As though whipped from beneath him, his elegantly booted feet now slipped uncontrollably and flew high into the air, while his buttocks (more bony and less cushioned than one might desire in such circumstances) made hard, dare one say crushing, contact with the frozen paving stones beneath. Thus cast down in such unforgiving fashion, his hat now fell off, taking with it his wig and exposing his hairless pate to the elements. Furthermore, his braces burst their buttons, a handful of gold sovereigns (one assumes to pay Mr. Jones for his Thermometer-repairing expertise) fell from his pocket, and his snuff box was ejected from his jacket, casting its contents into the filth of the cobblestones. The look of pain and shock on our dear friend's face at this moment would have to be seen to be believed, and the coldness for which no scientific proof is needed was clearly registered in his bones as acutely as it is for the rest of us mortals, but two most noteworthy details are worth describing. Firstly, that the Reverend made not one sound, not one cry of anguish, in any moment of this, his lips remaining firmly and resolutely closed. Secondly, his beloved Thermometer suffered no damage throughout, being thrust by his hand in perpendicular motion upwards as though by some animal instinct of protection, where it remained aloof and removed from the decline and fall below in which it had played no small part.

As for the poor Reverend, within a few moments he had managed to pick himself up, replace wig and hat to their rightful place, rebutton his braces and return the scattered coins to his pocket (the snuff and its box were left where they fell). Then, after a brief and vigorous rubbing of his affected parts, made to proceed with his journey, far more gingerly this time, but clearly grateful that the Thermometer had suffered far less damage than himself.

Yet there is a third detail of the Event that I wish to describe: at no instant in any of this, not before or during or after, was the attention of any of the bystanders distracted from your caricatures displayed in the shop window. An elderly churchman losing his dignity in such comic manner would ordinarily cause great hilarity amongst onlookers, and indeed become the stuff of many a repeated anecdote told and retold even by those who had not witnessed the spectacle themselves. Yet in this instance no one – not one person (except myself) – saw the Event, despite its happening right next to the crowd, because they were so distracted and amused at that very moment by your work – caricatures which, in numerous cases, show comic and satirical events not unlike the one which was taking place behind their backs. Not even the clinking of coins, or their golden shine as they spilled from the Reverend's pockets, was enough for their attention to be drawn.

My dear Mr. Gillray, do you see what you have done? You have portrayed the world so well and in such a palatable form, making it a colourful place of wit and laughter, that people no longer see the humdrum everyday variety; they can only see your version of it, and if an event does not appear in one of your illustrations then it does not exist for them at all – not even the kind of event which might otherwise appear in your caricatures.

Which inevitably, I believe, raises an interesting question: what is real? The Event? Or the caricature of it? Or a caricature (and here we get to the rub of the matter, and perhaps the subject of a new work) showing the Event taking place in the vicinity of people who are unaware of its passing because they are too absorbed in looking at caricatures depicting very similar Events? The truly curious thing is that, in turn, these people – potential witnesses, yet entirely ignorant of what has happened beneath their very noses – will only become aware of the Event because one day it will appear in the form of a caricature in the same window which distracted them from perceiving its passing in the first place, and all the while, behind them, further Events may still be happening…

I could go on, but shall stop there. Once one turns one's mind to such possibilities the logical twists can become dizzying and possibly fruitless, but I suspect by now that you see what I mean. Perhaps this cold snap has befuddled my own brain and you do not find this as curious and noteworthy as I, but on your return, if you so desire, we will talk about it further and I can provide you with more details.

I will end this letter here. It is late and I must to bed.

I wish you God speed.

Affectionately,
Mrs. Humphrey

The Arabian Nights Adventures

Tahir Shah

OVERCOME WITH RAGE, the monarch leapt up.

Hands clapping like cymbals, he bellowed at the top of his lungs for the royal guard. Crossing the room, he raised his fist to strike his bride, Scheherazade. But, as he swung in her direction, the grains of sand in the hourglass froze.

Down in the city below, nothing moved, the world paused freeze-frame.

In the teahouses, customers sat mid-conversation, rigid like statues. In their homes, families were motionless. Above the streets, birds hung in the night air, as though time had come to an end.

In the king's private apartment, the shadow of the Blue Witch roamed across the wall. Approaching Scheherazade, who was frozen as all the rest, she admonished the monarch for forcing such sorrow on his people. Then, whispering a spell, she cast a fistful of powdered antimony at the fire.

An explosion of light tore through the royal apartment.

Time and space were shunted on their axes, the silken walls melting into parched wilderness.

A sun hung like a great golden orb above an infinite desert. At the centre of the wasteland lay a secret caravanserai – a jumbled mess of tents plagued by flies, heat, and death.

On the northerly horizon, a dot was moving fitfully, like a flea vaulting about on a donkey's back. Gradually, it could be seen as what it was – a traveller riding a horse full tilt, as though his life depended on a message getting through.

Every few strides, his steed would buck and rear and, all too often, he would be thrown off, having to lure the poor creature back to him, and clamber on once again.

Due south of the encampment, a short, stout man was running through the sands, clothing shredded, his face a raw mask of desperation.

As the sun slipped to the edge of the earth, the two travellers reached the caravanserai and made their way to the one and only teahouse, with coarse carpets laid around it.

At the precise instant the two travellers arrived, the sound of a colossal bird high above drowned out the clamour of despondent camels.

Peering up into the last strains of dusk, the travellers watched as a young man tumbled from the clutches of a roc. He bounced onto the canopy of a goat-hair tent, and was thrown on the carpets laid outside the teahouse – landing between the other two travellers.

'That was close,' the young man said, checking himself for injuries.

'What magic caused you to be up there in the heavens?' the stout traveller said in awe.

'Hitching a ride, that's all.'

'From where?'

'From way over there, across the desert. Only a madman would attempt it on foot.'

'I came by horse,' the other traveller stated arrogantly.

'So I saw… You kept falling off!'

Recoiling in annoyance, the haughty traveller scowled.

'That's because I'm a sailor, and the desert I navigate is the ocean.'

The stout traveller pulled a scroll from his robe.

'I was ordered to come to this far-flung fragment of torment at this exact day and time.'

The sailor flinched.

'So was I,' he said, pulling a scroll from his saddlebag.

'And I,' said the young man who'd tumbled from the sky.

With no explanation why, the three travellers realized they'd each been ordered to arrive by dusk on the appointed day.

The traveller who'd come on foot explained that curiosity had brought him there.

The sailor echoed the reasoning.

The young man shrugged.

'Well, I'm afraid to reveal why I came,' he said. 'Whoever wrote the message said they would turn me in to the royal guard for a certain misdemeanour.'

Just then, a woman's voice spoke from the gathering darkness:

'Each one of you has been summoned here for the same reason. Although your reasons for agreeing to come differ.'

'Curiosity,' said the first.

'Exactly, the same,' intoned the second.

'Nonsense,' said the voice. 'Sindbad the Sailor, you came because I threatened to reveal your darkest secret to the Emperor of Cathay. And Ali Baba, you are here because I threatened to expose *your* secret to a certain sovereign – the one who's blind in the left eye. As for you, Aladdin, the list of your misdemeanours is so long there isn't a judge for a thousand horizons who wouldn't lock you up as soon as look at you!'

The three travellers squinted into the approaching night, trying to make out where the voice was coming from.

'It's a phantom,' said Sindbad.

'It's a jinn,' whispered Ali Baba.

'It's a woman!' hissed Aladdin.

'Two of you are wrong,' said the voice, 'and one is right.'

The sound of someone clearing their throat caused the three travellers to turn. Silhouetted against the campfire was the outline of a woman.

'Hello Sindbad, Ali Baba, and Aladdin,' she said. 'Consider yourselves introduced.'

'Who are you?' the sailor shot back.

'I am Scheherazade,' she said.

As the travellers quenched their thirst and feasted on a meal of roasted goat, the queen explained why they'd been summoned.

'Despite your varied lives and adventures, the three of you are heroes in a collection of tales… the greatest treasury of stories ever set down by humankind.'

Aladdin peered at Scheherazade through the campfire's flames.

'What's its name?' he asked.

'It's called *The Thousand and One Nights*,' the queen replied. 'Or, rather, it will become known as that. You see, the story has not yet been told – so its very existence hangs in the balance, as does mine.'

'How so?'

'Because, unless the telling continues,' Scheherazade explained, 'my life, and those of countless other queens, will be snuffed out as sure as night follows day.'

Aladdin pushed a hand back through his hair.

'Don't know about the others, but I'm not a character from a storyland,' he said. 'I'm a man who has a past and a future.'

The queen rolled her eyes.

'That's what *you* think,' she said. 'Of course you had no idea of who or what you really are, just as you had no notion of each other's existence – or that my voice, guided by certain forces, has conjured you, and shaped each one of your tales.'

Tossing down a mutton bone, Ali Baba spoke for the others:

'If you're not a jinn, then what are you?'

'I am a queen – a queen married to a ruthless king. If the tale I tell falters, as it has apparently done, he'll execute me, and a thousand more women.'

Sindbad reached for another morsel of meat.

'And why should it have faltered?' he said. 'After all, a story's a story and no more than that.'

Scheherazade peered out into the darkness, her mind reliving the predicament in which she found herself.

'The story's been diverted by a sorcerer in the employ of the king. He's thrown it out of kilter. As a result, the only certainty is my appointment with the executioner and his axe at dawn. Once I'm gone, King Shahriyar will marry a fresh bride each sunset and bury her each morning.'

Aladdin frowned.

'In what way has the story been disturbed?'

Scheherazade sighed.

'In our love for tales, we overlook how they work,' she said.

'They work because a storyteller speaks, and someone listens. It's as simple as that.'

'No,' the queen replied. 'If that were true, then we wouldn't be in the quandary we're in. You see, when a tale is begun, a seed is planted, a seed from which the story grows and grows. Sometimes the seed ripens into a little story – no more than a handful of words. But, at other times, it matures into a fantastical reflection of wonder.'

'What's the seed got to do with any of us?' Ali Baba asked.

'All three of you are heroes in a vast and intricate tale, a story that's a labyrinth of astonishment – the most complex tale ever told. Although I have only just begun recounting it, the twists, turns, and each individual adventure is contained within the story seed. Hide the seed, and the tale goes awry.'

'How would anyone hide a story's seed?' Sindbad snapped. 'It sounds preposterous, as though it were out of a story itself!'

'Of course it sounds as though it's from a story,' Scheherazade cried, 'because it *is*! As for how the seed of a story can be hidden, it's achieved through supernatural means. In this case, by the King of the Jinns.'

The sailor winced.

'I wish you luck,' he said. 'But I have a voyage to attend to.'

'And I have a shop to run,' Ali Baba mumbled.

'If you don't help me,' said the queen, 'I could have you both thrown into the deepest, darkest dungeon in any one of a dozen kingdoms.'

Silence prevailed, eventually broken by Aladdin:

'Nothing would please me more than to be part of your quest,' he said with a smile.

Begrudgingly, the other two agreed, too.

'Excellent,' Scheherazade said. 'We leave at dawn.'

'Where to?' the sailor asked.

'To the City of Brass!'

Long before the first blush of desert light warmed the travellers' faces, Scheherazade woke the others one by one.

During the few hours of rest, dreams transported them far from the freezing, flea-infested caravanserai.

Sindbad dreamt he was in a palace in distant China.

Aladdin imagined he was in a fantastical treasure cave.

Ali Baba fantasized he would one day own the most colossal marketplace for goods from all corners of the world.

Before setting out, Scheherazade explained the City of Brass was the destination because the kindly Blue Witch had revealed it was from there that the story's seed had been taken. On hearing the information, Sindbad clenched his hands into fists.

'You speak of witches, and claim to have power over us,' he said, straightening his back imperiously, 'but how do we know your power until we've seen it?!'

Scheherazade rolled her eyes.

'I am the teller of the story, of *your* story,' she replied. 'So I can control each one of you as I wish.'

With that, she pointed to the sailor.

'And the queen pointed to Sindbad,' she said, 'her right hand clenched as a fist. Twisting it, she caused him to raise from the ground and turn in mid-air, hanging there like a bird in flight.'

As she spoke, Sindbad rose from the ground, and turned upside down.

'Put me down!' he cried.

'With pleasure,' said Scheherazade.

Clicking her fingers, the sailor fell headfirst onto the sand.

Ali Baba stepped forward.

'Your Magnificence,' he said, fawning, 'I would be most obliged if you wouldn't use such necromancy ever in our presence.'

Aladdin and Sindbad seconded the request.

'Are you certain that's your wish?' Scheherazade said.

The three travellers nodded in unison.

'Please swear it in an oath,' they said all at once.

'Very well. I, Scheherazade, reluctant wife of King Shahriyar, pledge on all I hold sacred that while in your presence I shan't use the powers at my disposal as a storyteller.'

With that, the procession pushed out of the caravanserai.

As the first rays of dawn light broke across the horizon, three dozen camels moved over the vast emptiness, a giant shadow thrown by each one.

Scheherazade led the way, the travellers behind her, and a retinue of pack animals and their attendants following at the rear. The frail light of dawn was quickly replaced by the piercing blaze of late morning, and heat so intense that it scorched any skin left unprotected.

Their heads furled in turbans, the ends tied over their faces, the humans were hopelessly prepared for life in the parched wasteland.

Time and again Sindbad lost his balance and fell from his mount, to the amusement of the others.

'I'm a man of the sea!' he bawled. 'Put me on the ocean and you will know my skill.'

The sailor may have been unsure in his footing, but his aptitude for navigation was second to none. Charting the way by the night sky, he pointed out the constellations to the others, regaling them at the nightly campfire with tales of his voyages.

'I have crossed seas with waves as great as mountains,' he said, 'and with whales that would swallow an entire ship if they had the will. I've sailed to the ends of the earth, swum with mermaids, and listened to the cries of the great *bahamut*, the immense sea creature which holds up the earth.'

'And what did you learn in all your adventures?' asked Scheherazade.

The sailor didn't reply at first. He stared into the embers, his mind zigzagging through all the narrow escapes.

'I learned to treat every day as the greatest wonder imaginable,' he answered.

Aladdin wiped a hand down over his youthful face.

'And what have *you* learned in your adventures?' he asked the queen.

She smiled.

'To understand the power of stories,' she said.

The Arabian Carpet and the Land of No Magic

Jason Webster

THE CALIPH'S DAUGHTER was terribly ill, and after all the physicians in the land had tried and failed to heal her, the court magician was summoned.

'Cure the princess!' ordered the caliph. 'Or lose your head.'

The magician tried all manner of tricks and potions, but to no avail.

'Nothing can cure her, Majesty,' said the magician, trembling at the caliph's feet. 'She has been called to the invisible world; it is her time.'

'Nonsense!' cried the caliph. Yet as the poor magician was being dragged away, news arrived that the princess had indeed breathed her last.

For forty days the caliph locked himself in his rooms. After the death of his wife, his daughter had been his only joy. Now that she, too, had gone, all light had left his world.

On the day that his official mourning ended, he ordered the captain of the guard to come to him.

'Send your men out to every corner of the empire,' he said. 'Find every magician, every fakir, every wizard, every sorcerer and every person engaged in those nefarious arts, and throw them into gaol. And there they can rot while we decide what to do with them.'

The captain carried out his orders with great diligence: every practitioner of magic had their wands and other tools of sorcery seized and, powerless as a result, were cast in chains. Soon, not a single one was at liberty.

Years passed. The empire became known as the Land of No Magic. Most people's lives carried on much the same, but something subtle and important – something no one could quite put their finger on – was missing.

The caliph himself, however, was content.

'No more magic, no more misery,' he would say to himself every morning as he looked out from the palace window. 'Besides, they're all charlatans anyway.'

Now with all the magicians incapacitated, there was nothing anyone could do to bring magic back into the empire. Yet in issuing his order, the caliph had missed one important category: magic carpets. These were still at large, if maintaining a low profile.

Yet realizing that the fate of magic itself now rested with them, the carpets held an extraordinary assembly.

'Even our weavers have been imprisoned,' said the eldest when they all gathered in the shadow of a sacred, snow-capped mountain. 'If we do nothing, magic itself will cease to exist. There is only one thing for it: we must find the master weaver, he who created the very first of us. None other than Eight Fingers himself!'

'But where can we find him?' cried the assembled carpets. 'We don't even know what Eight Fingers looks like.'

'His whereabouts are unknown to anyone but himself,' said the ancient carpet. 'We must fly to every corner until we find him. For only he can restore order to the world.'

Now one of the carpets present was a young Arabian who heard these words and with youthful determination swore not to rest until Eight Fingers had been located.

Every night, when the people in its home were asleep, the carpet would set off into the starlit sky in search of the mysterious master.

But very soon the magic carpets themselves were in danger: sightings had been made of them as they criss-crossed the horizon in their quest, and in a rage, the caliph – believing he had eradicated all magic from his lands – ordered them to be hunted down. One by one the carpets were caught by the royal guards using nets, cannons, and all manner of means to bring them back to earth. And before long, the only magic carpet still evading capture was the young Arabian.

'It's up to me!' it said, as it set off once more on its search.

High above the moonlit desert it soared, but that night it, too, was spotted, and the captain of the royal guard sent up a new weapon – a flying machine – to capture it.

The Arabian swooped and swerved in the air to escape, flying low to the ground in the hope that it might find somewhere to hide. Before long, it spied a cave in a mountainside. Diving into it, it tightened itself into as small a roll as it could.

The captain of the guard, however, was in pursuit, and set a squadron of his best men to scour the landscape and bring the carpet to him.

Soon the soldiers were clambering all over the rocks, and before long one of them had spotted the cave.

'Perhaps it's down there,' said the guard to his sergeant. Deep inside the cave, the Arabian curled itself into an ever-tighter roll, hoping against hope to remain unseen.

'Fool!' said the sergeant. 'Look, there's a spider's web covering the entrance. There's no way it's down there.'

The guard looked, and there, indeed, was a spider's web stretching unbroken from one side to the other. And so the soldiers moved on.

Deep in the cave, the Arabian heard this, not believing its luck. And once it was safe to do so, it unrolled itself and peeped up towards the entrance. Lo and behold, it saw that there was indeed a large spider sitting at the middle of a great web covering the hole. And as a shaft of moonlight beamed down on it, the Arabian saw the web transform into a rich tapestry of bright colours and designs, more beautiful than anything it had ever seen. The spider raised one leg as if to show the carpet, then another and another and another.

'One, two, three...' the Arabian counted. '... Seven, eight. Eight fingers!' it cried. 'You are Eight Fingers! I have found you!'

The Arabian quickly told the master weaver everything that had happened, about the princess, the caliph, and the order against magic.

'I can help,' said Eight Fingers. 'But you must do exactly as I say.'

The Arabian promised, and so the spider climbed onto its back, buried himself in its woollen fibres, and together they took off into the night sky.

Now the next night, in the royal palace, the caliph was in his bedchamber getting ready to go to sleep when he looked down and saw a carpet by the bed.

'That's strange,' he said to himself. 'I don't remember seeing that there before.'

He was about to order it to be taken away, when he thought that, actually, he rather liked it, that its colours and patterns were pleasing to him, and decided it should stay.

Just then, as he was standing on it, dressed only in his bed robes and about to pull back the sheets, the carpet rose into the air and as quick as a flash carried him out the open window and high above the city.

'Help!' cried the caliph. But they were so high up that no one could hear him.

Far into the night sky and over the distant horizon they flew. At first the caliph closed his eyes and curled into a ball, hoping it was just a nightmare. But every time he opened them, there he was still, on the carpet, soaring through the air as though it were the most natural thing in the world.

Clinging to the edge for dear life, he peered over and saw strange lands below, territories far beyond his own realms; mountains so tall that they touched the sky; lush green forests that stretched in every direction; vast oceans wider than his eyes could see filled with amazing and monstrous creatures.

'No more!' cried the caliph, petrified with fear. 'No more!'

And with that, he woke up with a start, lying in his own bed, with the sun just beginning to rise.

Thank Heavens for that, he thought to himself. It was nothing but a dream.

The next night, however, when he was getting ready for sleep, as he stepped onto the carpet the same thing happened again. Up it rose and out the window they flew. This time the caliph saw new wonders from on high: enormous cities inhabited by peoples he had never seen before, with magnificent temples and palaces far greater than his own. And although he was still frightened, and clung to the edge of the carpet until his knuckles went white, he gazed more intently at what he saw.

These people seem much happier than my own, he thought to himself. They are more prosperous and clearly love their ruler more than my people love me.

But before he could reflect any more, he found himself back in his bed, with the sun rising once more in the east.

On and on this continued every night. Directed by Eight Fingers, the Arabian carpet would transport the caliph to the distant corners of the earth, and on its travels showed him marvels far beyond his imagination. But the caliph also saw misery and suffering where it, too, was to be found. And he wept as powerfully as he rejoiced at the wonders before him.

Seven nights passed like this in which the caliph saw more than most people see in several lifetimes. On the eighth night, as he was getting ready for bed once more, he stood on the carpet and this time spoke to it.

'I know now that this is no dream,' he said. 'You are a magic carpet and I know that you have been transporting me to distant lands every night. Now it is my desire that you should carry me where *I* wish to go. Henceforth, you shall obey my commands!'

Instead, however, the carpet simply rose into the night air once more and whisked the caliph away. This time, rather than travelling to far horizons, it stayed within the empire and visited, one by one, all the prisons where the magicians and wizards that had been locked up so many years before were still languishing, many of them now close to death.

And the caliph, confronted by the sight of them, grieved at what he had done, and wept more bitterly than before.

The next morning, when he woke up, he called for the captain of the guard and ordered the release of every man and woman who had been gaoled for practising magic.

'Henceforth,' an imperial decree declared, 'all magic carried out for the purposes of good is permitted. Magic is no longer forbidden.'

The people rejoiced and danced in the street at the news. And before long, as the magicians and sorcerers and witches came back to live among them, they noticed that something subtle and important – something they couldn't quite put their finger on – had somehow returned to their lives.

And the caliph himself noticed it. He still mourned for his wife and daughter, but from now on did everything in his power to make sure his people could be as happy as possible.

As for the Arabian carpet, well, the caliph went back to his chambers to look for it, but it had vanished. And they say that from that day on it has continued to fly with Eight Fingers to all four corners of the world, bringing a touch of magic back into the lives of those who most need it.

Nasrudin: Shadowman

Tahir Shah

NASRUDIN WENT FOR a haircut in a side street near the Galata
Tower in Istanbul.

Having left his suitcase just inside the door, he sat down
on the chair. Within a minute or two, the barber had got
down to work with his scissors. He cocked his head over to
the luggage.

'So, are you travelling alone?'

'Oh no,' Nasrudin responded, 'Anwar's with me.'

'Who's Anwar... your son?'

'No, my shadow.'

The barber frowned.

'But a shadow isn't a person... so it can't have a name.'

The wise fool shrugged.

'Who says a shadow can't have a name?'

'Because they don't.'

'Yes, they do. In my homeland all the shadows have
names.'

'Really?'

'Yes.'

After lifetime of cutting hair, the barber had heard all kinds of tall tales, but never anything so strange as shadows having names.

Silence prevailed for a while.

Then, rekindling the conversation, the barber sniffed.

'So, tell me, what's the population of people in your country?'

Nasrudin narrowed his eyes.

'With or without shadows?' he asked.

Finis